Lyonne Riley

Hallow's Cove is a charming small town at the juncture of mountain and sea, originally founded nearly a century ago as a refuge for the supernatural. Now occupied primarily by monsters, Hallow's Cove has become a destination for tourists of all kinds who seek to enjoy hiking, skiing, swimming, and more. Visit at any time of year to experience this quaint, old-fashioned town and all the fun activities and natural beauty it has to offer!

Twilight Peak
Hallow's Hill Ski Resort
Beacon Beach
Barnaby's Manse
Beatrice Memorial
Kasper Bay
Kasper Marina
Downtown
Haffman's Farm

Hallow's Cove School
Town Hall
Ice Rink
Cool Beans Cafe
Cafe
Info Center
Cove Arts Centre
Motel
Bodega
Rick's Hardware
Coming Up Daisies
Bookstore
Thrift Shop
Gargoyle's Games
Green Grocer
Deja Hairdo

Story Introduction

AFTER MAKING A BIG mistake at work, Maisie is told to take a mandatory vacation and get her head on straight. But when she chooses Hallow's Cove as her retreat destination, she doesn't realize it's a town inhabited almost purely by monsters—including her grumpy new landlord, Barnaby.

It's no secret that Barnaby the bookstore owner is a vampire, but he's long since tamed his urge to drink human blood. That is, until Maisie arrives in Hallow's Cove. Her blood smells utterly wonderful, and Barnaby finds himself drawn to her scent just as much as he is to her genuine, curious personality.

But Barnaby fears his attraction, too, because he carries a secret: inside every vampire is a monster, one that's never been seen or written about. The closer he gets to Maisie, the higher the risk that it could escape containment. When sparks fly between them, will the hidden creature emerge and ruin his chance at love?

Content Warnings

- Blood play

- Graphic depictions of sex

- Shifted/monster sex

- Killing (off-screen)

- On-screen death and rebirth

Chapter One

Maisie

A SHARP CHIRP FROM my phone wakes me out of a dead sleep.

> Maisie, we need to talk. ASAP.

I blink bleary eyes at my phone screen. No one ever messages me on the work Slack before ten a.m., especially not after last night. They all know I was awake until four making final bug fixes on our new release, and I'm grumpy and foul-tempered if I'm bothered early.

I slide out of bed, throw on pajama pants and a nice shirt, and slide into my computer chair. In my reflection on the black screen, I can see my curly hair is a wild mess, so I quickly tidy it before logging in to my work VPN.

Immediately, the ring of a video call from my boss, Wade, blasts my eardrums.

"What's up?" I ask, trying to keep the sleepiness out of my voice but failing miserably.

Wade does not look pleased. "The network crashed," he says in a clipped tone. "Something you did last night destabilized it. We were supposed to have a release today, and instead, none of the players can log in."

Staring at him through the screen, I play back in my memory what I did last night. I was crushing the last two bugs on the list, bugs nobody else had gotten around to fixing before they were all dead on their feet. But I kept going until the early hours of the morning to make sure everything was tip-top perfect before the new update rolled out to our users.

"When I logged out last night, everything was working fine!" Bile rises in my throat. There's no way I made a mistake big enough to take out the entire network. It's not possible.

"The moment the release hit, everything went down." Wade's expression is as hard as stone. "What can you remember?"

Tears bite at the back of my eyes as I comb through my memory, but nothing stands out. I had plenty of Red Bull and coffee in my system, so it wasn't like I was falling asleep at the wheel. It actually took me forever to finally pass out once I had finished the last of it because I was so buzzed on caffeine.

"I'm so sorry," is all I can manage, my eyes growing heavy and wet. Wade's tough demeanor falls and his shoulders sag.

"Fuck, Maisie. Don't cry." His cat crawls into his lap. "I'm sure it was a mistake—"

"I don't make mistakes like that!" Fuck, now I really am crying. "I'm sorry, Wade. I'll fix it right now. I'll figure out what went wrong, no problem."

"No."

The gruff word stops me short. I stare into the webcam perched on the top of my monitor, wondering why he won't let me fix what I broke.

"What?" I blanch. "But—"

"I said 'no'!" Wade's tone is harsher than I've ever heard him before, and I want to crawl into a hole and die. "You've done enough. I've already put other engineers on fixing the problem, and they'll handle it."

"But I can fix it!" I must seem pathetic right now, but the worst punishment I could imagine is someone else having to hunt down my sloppy bug. I'm good at my job, I know what I'm doing, and I was certain that everything was working perfectly when I went to bed last night. I would never have let myself rest otherwise.

"Go back to bed, Maisie," Wade says firmly. "We're going to have a talk later, once this is all put back together."

Then the call goes dead. I crumple in my chair, my face in my hands as tears stream down my face. Of course I won't be able to sleep after that, so when I climb under my blankets, I lie there staring at the ceiling and wishing I could turn back time to figure out what went wrong.

Am I going to get fired?

When the call comes, I leap to my feet and scurry across the room to slide into my desk chair. It's Wade again.

Is this my last day? Is this the call that will send me packing after all the years and years I've put into *Swords of Malroth*?

"Hi," I say as he pops up on my screen. I will not cry in front of my boss a second time.

"The server is back up and running." He narrows his eyes at me. "And you are taking a vacation."

I stare at the screen. "What? But I don't have anything planned." I never take vacations. My work is my vacation, because I love what I do. I don't even know how I'd spend a day off.

"Consider it an order, Maisie. You need a reset. I can't have my best employee so burned out that she's making mistakes like this."

Don't cry. Don't cry. Don't cry.

"Oh," is all I manage to say. "I'm not burned out, though—"

"You're going." Wade's tone is firm and final. "I want you gone for a whole month this summer. And while you're off, we're going to conduct an investigation into what happened last night."

My heart plummets. "An investigation?" I squeeze my eyes shut, breathing hard to keep myself from breaking down.

Wade gives me a stern look. "And if you even log on once in the next month, you're fired."

My mouth falls open. What on earth will I do for an entire month? I play a lot of video games, but I can't occupy myself with only that.

"Go somewhere new," Wade suggests. "Get out of the house. Explore the world a little and get your head back on straight."

All I can do is nod. Despite our friendly relationship, I know he's serious about this.

"Fine." I sniffle. "A whole month, though? Really?"

"A whole month. Depending on the outcome of the investigation, I might let you come back sooner, but in the meantime, find some resort and treat yourself. Go traveling. There's more out there than this job."

But he doesn't understand. There isn't anything else out there for me.

When we sign off for the last time, I sit in my chair staring off into space. I already feel adrift.

With a heavy sigh, I open a new tab in my browser window. I don't have any pets, so leaving home for a month just means paying my rent in advance and turning off the gas. I'll need a place to stay if I'm leaving town, so I start there.

I browse listings for vacation homes within driving distance, all of them big, sprawling houses with fireplaces and astounding views. But I want something that will still feel like home—and something I can actually afford for that long.

"Entire apartment," one of the listings reads. It's a cute one-bedroom place with a kitchenette, living room, one bedroom and one bathroom. "Located in the beautiful small town of Hallow's Cove. Live right above a bookstore on Main Street and enjoy everything this scenic town has to offer."

I don't bother reading the description as I enter my dates, from tomorrow through next month, to see if it's available. It's a long shot, but who knows.

Sure enough, the apartment is open. This might be the only spot I can find on short notice, so I book it without a second look. Then I start packing.

Barnaby

What people will never really understand is the vast multitude of knowledge contained within books. All of humankind's accomplishments culminate in the book. It is a physical testament to the sharing and preservation of information throughout history, and the only true primary source from the past.

Well, I keep those particular books in the back room where I can protect them from grubby hands and mold. Up here in the front of the store I carry your standard fiction novels—some thrillers, some mystery, some romance. There's a small aisle of children's books, and behind them, the cookbooks and biographies. Up front, in the window, are the local guidebooks, maps, and information booklets. I also have a rather thorough selection of greeting cards, featuring grumpy old ladies and cute animals with funny tag lines. I like to keep a little bit of everything on hand, so people who visit from out of town have a decent selection of books for their hotel evenings.

Whenever I get new customers, though, I push the latest Anne Hadron release. That woman sure knows how to tell a sordid historical tale—but no one seems quite as interested as I am. I really admire how much research and thought she puts into her stories, and how accurate they are to a period of time most writers get wrong.

I would know, because I was there.

But usually visitors pick up a sudoku book, or some shallow thriller, so I always make sure to keep plenty of James Pierson on hand. As there's no cell phone coverage in Hallow's Cove, tourists are looking for something to keep them occupied.

Humans don't even realize that Google has scrambled their brains like eggs on toast. It's stolen their curiosity. Once upon a time, you had to pull a volume from your encyclopedia to answer a question, and you would learn all sorts of other marvelous things along the way.

It's been a nice, quiet day so far. I'm enjoying my latest backroom acquisition, a first-hand account of World War I, when the door to the shop flies open in a jingle of bells.

Mayor Louise strides in, all frilly collar and high heels, which only makes her maybe a few inches over five feet. She's a squat woman, roughly an apple shape, with a voice that makes my eardrums rattle.

"Barnaby!" She calls out my name as if we are long-lost friends. She strides over to the counter and taps it with her long nails. "I just wanted to check in and see how you're doing."

I don't look up from my book. "What do you want?"

She giggles. "Just as prickly as ever. Retract the fangs." She slaps a paper down on the counter, startling me so much I almost fall off my stool. "I have a wonderful idea for how to open tourist season this year!"

Oh, fabulous. Another Louise Idea.

I let out a weary sigh. "What is it this time?"

"A fair on Main Street! We would close off downtown to everyone but foot traffic, and shops would bring out their best wares and set them up on tables. We'll have face painting, bobbing for apples, all sorts of fun activities while promoting local businesses!"

I close my eyes and massage the bridge of my nose. "I do not want face painting and apple bobbing anywhere near my books, thank you." Kids with messy faces and sticky hands are exactly the kind of thing I try to keep far away from my merchandise. When children come into my shop, I watch them like a hawk, and quickly bring out the bleach wipes after they've left to clean off any books they touched.

"Well, you don't have to put your books out if you don't want to, Barnaby," Louise says, enthusiasm untainted. "You have cards, and puzzles—all sorts of things for visitors to enjoy! You could even open the other side of the store!"

She speaks like one of those obnoxious travel videos that plays at the hotel. *Here are all the fun things to do during your visit to Hallow's Cove!* It makes me want to stab myself in the ear.

I narrow my eyes at her. "I will not open the other side." It's too quiet and too dark, with too many fragile memories stored in it. "But... perhaps I will put out a puzzle. And some bookmarks."

"That's the spirit," Louise says brightly. "The idea is to welcome people in, show them the culture, and get a running start to a great tourist season!"

Why does every sentence of hers have to end with an exclamation mark?

"Fucking tourist season," I mutter as one of the sassy fridge magnets in the impulse buy section catches Louise's attention. "Nothing but bad traffic and bad customers."

The only upside to tourist season is it brings in most of the town's money. Without it, we wouldn't have much of an economy. I may loathe the sunburned tourists and their sticky offspring, but I'm also a realist, so I do my best to tolerate them since as many of the other residents rely on them to pay the bills.

The mayor *tsks* at my cursing. "Come now, Barnaby. Tourist season can be fun, too. There are so many new people to meet, and who knows what excitement some stranger might bring into your life?"

I physically flinch at the suggestion. The last thing I need is for some pain-in-my-ass summer tourist to take an interest in me. I'm much too old for that, and far too tired. So fucking tired.

That's when a new email pops up on the computer with a *ding!*

"You've got a booking!" the subject line reads. I have to read it a few times before I can even remember what it's about.

Right. I listed the apartment months ago, but nobody's attempted to rent it yet. The place is rather bare and certainly nothing to look at. The hotels all offer far better accommodations.

Hopefully it's only for a night or two. I don't know why I caved to Louise's bullying and listed the place. It was sitting empty, and eventually she convinced me it was wasteful.

"A *month*?" I ask with horror when I open the email and read the dates for the booking. I'm going to have to tolerate another person above my store for a whole month. A complete stranger, crossing paths with me who knows how many times a day? I wish I'd never put that godforsaken rental up.

This is all Louise's fault. Damn it.

She squeals and claps her hands as she reads the message over my shoulder. I didn't even notice she'd slipped around my counter.

"A tenant!" the mayor crows, and I glare at her. "That's great news! That place has been empty for a while, but a long-term visitor? This will be great for you, Barnaby."

I truly cannot imagine anything worse.

Chapter Two

Maisie

AFTER I'VE CHUCKED TWO weeks' worth of clothes into a suitcase, I pack up my laptop, charger, and cell phone and shove it all in my car. I picked a rental apartment somewhere close enough that I could drive in a few hours because I hate flying more than anything. Waking up early to get to the airport? Standing like cattle in security lines? Wedged into too-small seats next to total strangers? No thanks.

I recently upgraded my ride, and I'm glad I did. It's a fancy new electric car with tons of gadgets inside. It has cameras everywhere, and the built-in AI system can even take over the wheel on the highway. I'll have to keep an eye on it, of course, to make sure it does what it's supposed to do—but the rest of the time I'll be able to sit back, relax, and enjoy the drive to the tune of an audiobook. I chose a pulp thriller this time, something mindless to occupy me during the four-hour drive into the mountains and toward the coast. Before I hop in the car, I shoot a text to my parents and my brother about where I'm headed—though I carefully leave out the reason why.

Once I'm on the highway, I set my car to autopilot and turn on the audiobook. It's just as engaging as I'd hoped, even though the quality of the writing leaves something to be desired. But it makes the hours fly by, and thanks to my new fancy car, I get to watch the scenery along the way, which slightly dulls the ache of this forced vacation.

As I get closer and closer to my destination, though, the signal on my phone cuts in and out. Baffled, I turn it off and restart it, hoping it's just a blip. But the signal is only getting worse. By the time I reach the city limits and take over driving again, there's no service at all.

I was expecting some kind of hiccup with my cellular provider since I live in the city, so I pull over at a scenic stop and pop out my SIM card, then replace it with another one that might get better service here.

Still nothing.

I try another SIM card, my last one, and no dice. Not a single provider gets reception way out here. Is there not even a cell tower in town?

I grow worried as I start the car again and drive past the huge sign reading WELCOME TO HALLOW'S COVE! Population: 4,592.

Yeah, it's a tiny place, but it should still get cell service, right?

Shit. I didn't write down the address of the apartment where I'm staying, thinking I'd just be able to pull it up on the phone app once I got here. It had instructions for check-in and everything. I'm going to have to find internet and do it on my computer instead.

I drive slowly down Main Street, looking for a coffee shop that might have Wi-Fi. It's the quaintest, cutest little town I've ever seen. Pretty awnings decorate the fronts of shops, and it all looks like something out of a different time. The 1950s, maybe.

Not great for getting cell coverage.

Eventually I find a window with a huge coffee cup on it and pull into a parking spot on the main drag. Inside, I check around for a sheet of paper with a Wi-Fi password on it.

"Can I help you?" someone asks from behind the counter. When I glance up, I find a huge, two-legged wolf staring down at me. He's got pointy brown ears, a long snout, and a wet nose that shines under the lights. I stare at him for far too long, and he blinks back at me.

"Um..." I finally manage to recover my senses. I've never seen a wolven in person before. "Do you have internet here?"

He nods. "Yep! I'll write the password on your cup."

Ah, yeah. I need to be a customer first. "All right. I'll take a coffee, black, the strongest you've got. Thank you."

I pay, and then wait as the big wolf busies about making my pour-over coffee. I'm amazed his claws don't get in the way. When he hands me the cup, I find "PASSWORD" written across it.

"That's not very secure," I say, frowning.

The wolven sighs. "I know, but if we set it to anything else, people can't remember it."

Right, it is a tourist town. They probably get a lot of space cadets in here.

I quickly take the cup, pull out my laptop, and connect. The internet's mind-numbingly slow, but eventually I get access to my email and the website that has my reservation.

"Hallow's Cove is a town inhabited mostly by monsters," the description says, a little farther down.

Ah. I missed that part completely. There are monsters everywhere in the world, of course, but they're typically few and far between. A whole town of them will make for an interesting vacation.

I jot down the address and check-in instructions, which involve going into the bookstore and asking for the owner. Simple enough.

Buoyed by this small success, I slug down half of my coffee, dump the other half, and get back into my car. I drive another block or two until I spot a store with books arranged in the window.

Perfect.

Again I park out front, pleased at how much easier it is to find parking here than in the city. I hop out and head into the store, and the bells jingle as I step inside the darkness.

Wow. Yeah. It's really dark in here.

"Hello?" Because it was so bright outside, I can barely see.

"What do you need?" asks a gruff voice.

Finally, with one eye closed, I can make out the shelves lining the store, and the tall human man sitting behind the counter with a book open in his lap. He has dark hair that's slicked back, with shocks of gray around his temples that tell me he's likely in his late forties. His face is long and slender with a pronounced chin and nose. There's a regal quality to him, like he's from another time completely. He's even dressed in a vest that hugs his slim but muscular frame, with a collared shirt underneath and a red tie.

"Oh. Hi. Sorry. I booked the apartment? Upstairs?" I offer my widest, most radiant smile. "I just need help getting access to it, and then I'll leave you alone."

The man's dark eyes widen, and then his lips twist in disgust. "Right."

I don't think he's very pleased about having his reading time interrupted. He gets out of his chair slowly, then sighs and grabs some keys. Without another word, he leads me out of the store to a door not four feet from the shop entrance. Slipping the key into the ancient lock, he turns it and a mechanism on the other side creaks. Then he pushes the door open for me.

"Here you are." The words are polite, but the tone of voice is impatient. "Enjoy your stay."

With that, he walks away.

"Wait!" I call out. He pauses and turns to me with an irritable look. I hope I don't need to ask him for too many more things during my stay here, because I think it'll be just as unpleasant. "The key? I need that, probably."

"Oh, right." He grumbles as he unhooks the key from his keychain, then presses it into my hand. His skin is shockingly cold, as if he's been in a refrigerator.

"I haven't been able to get a signal here," I say. "So I'm not sure how to contact you."

The man frowns. "Why would you need to contact me?"

"Uh…" I flounder. "I don't know, in case something goes wrong?"

That intense look of his grows even more suspicious. "What would go wrong?"

"I don't know!" We've only just met and he's already driving me crazy. "Anything could happen. I need to be able to get a hold of you, though."

"Then pick up the phone." He gestures up at the apartment. "My number is written next to it."

I stare as I try to make sense of this. Finally, it dawns on me.

"Oh, a landline?"

He *hmphs*. "Yes. A landline. Cell phones don't work in Hallow's Cove."

"What?" I look down at the phone in my hand. "What do you mean? That's impossible. Everyone has cell service nowadays—"

"We don't. There's Wi-Fi here, and at the coffee shop, and a few other places in town. There are landlines if you need to call out, but you'll have to pay extra for long distance." With a finality, he turns around and departs back to the bookstore, slamming the door closed behind him.

I stand there, dumbstruck, for far too long. Shit. Have I made a mistake with the place I chose to stay? This guy is probably the most unfriendly person I've ever met.

He didn't appear to be a monster, though. I wonder if perhaps he's a shifter, like our old systems administrator. She could turn into a bear at will, which was comical when she got surprised by her pet cat on a company-wide call and transformed there on screen.

Hopefully I won't need to ask him for help anytime soon.

Grabbing a bag from my car, I head up the narrow, rickety stairs to the apartment. It's got a surprising amount of light coming in through the front windows, and it's clean, but also completely empty. There's a cute kitchen, big enough for one person to move about comfortably, though there isn't a table or chairs to speak of. The living room has nothing in it except a small television mounted on the wall.

I check the first closed door down the hall to discover a bedroom, which contains a bed on an old metal frame. The other door holds a tiny bathroom with a shower stall, sink, and toilet. There's a single towel and a washcloth sitting on the tank.

I walk back into the empty living room, puzzled. He must be kidding. There's nowhere to sit and eat, or watch the television, or really to do anything.

This is ridiculous. I can't stay here.

On the counter that divides the living room and the kitchen is the phone that the landlord mentioned. I didn't even get his name.

"Bookstore," I read aloud. It's written on a piece of paper taped to the counter next to the phone, with a seven-digit phone number. Not even an area code.

I pick up the phone and dial. It rings twice before someone answers with a deep sigh.

"Hello. Bookstore." It's the same man as before, and he sounds very irritated.

"Um, hi, yeah. I'm the tenant that just arrived."

"Yes, and?"

"*And* there's no furniture up here."

The other end of the line is silent, and I have to check to make sure it's still connected.

"Is anyone there?" I ask when no reply comes.

"Yes, yes." Another bone-weary sigh. "What sort of *furniture* do you need?"

The way he says it, like what I'm asking is a major inconvenience, grates on my nerves.

"Somewhere to sit while I eat, for starters," I say. "A bar stool for the counter? A table? A chair? A sofa? You know, things normal people need."

"Fine. I have some things. Come downstairs."

Then the call ends with a *beep*. I glare down at it. This was supposed to be a vacation, but already I want to turn around and go home. Maybe I should. I could always pretend I went somewhere, then just sit and play video games for the next four weeks.

No. I set the phone back into its cradle firmly. I'm not going to let some weird asshole scare me off. I paid to come here and stay in this apartment. The least he can do is give me a chair to sit on.

I stalk back down the stairs, clutching the key in my pocket. If this guy's going to be a dick to me, I have two choices: I can kill him with kindness, or I can be a dick right back.

Given that his shop is right next door, I'll probably have to see him often. The last thing I want is animosity with the first person—no, the second person—I've met in town.

It's decided. I'll be as sweet as I can and try to make my next four weeks enjoyable. As if that's even possible without cell phone service.

Chapter Three

Barnaby

OH, I CAN ALREADY tell the new tenant is going to be a severe pain in my ass. The words are written right there on the wall. First she wants furniture, which means opening up the storage room. Then what? A coffee maker? Mugs?

Humans need so many things, and it's all going to cost me.

I should never have listed that stupid apartment. This is all Louise's fault. My preference would have been to let the loft collect dust and cobwebs, but she's right in that it's valuable Main Street real estate.

"Someone should enjoy this place," she'd said. "All that good light and a view of downtown? It's a prime location."

Now I'm going to be stuck with this demanding human for an entire month.

But then there's the other thing. The fact that she smelled... absolutely, incredibly delectable. Like the fullest, sweetest fruit, and I have never, ever encountered someone who smelled that close to heaven.

The scent had floated over to me when she came inside and neared the desk. There are only a few smells in the world that trigger my taste buds, and at the very top of the list is human blood.

All humans, though, smell the same. Blood, blood, everywhere. Fresh blood fueling a beating heart is the most delicious of all the world's delicacies. Nothing I tasted in my human life compares to the flavor, and I will spend the remainder of my eternity longing for it.

This woman's blood, though, smells absolutely marvelous. It washed over me when she waltzed into my store, and my fangs extruded inside my mouth at just the hint of it beneath her skin. The promise of it had nearly overwhelmed me. I am only lucky that my true form cannot emerge during the day, or I might have simply changed there in front of her in my surprise.

I'm left wondering after she leaves why she smelled like succulent perfection. Why did this one woman trigger my hunger in a way no one has in all my life as a vampire?

As we head to the back of the bookstore, I take stock of her again. She has curly, fierce reddish-orange hair that makes it look like her head is on fire. Her eyes are hazel and shockingly large in her little freckled face. Unlike most young people I see, though, she's dressed like a much older woman, with long pants, a baggy blouse, and a cardigan over the top that fully disguises the shape of her body.

The woman meekly follows along behind me as I stop at the old door at the rear of the shop and fish another key out of my pocket. I wish I had other options besides showing her this place, but unless I'm willing to mail out for a bunch of brand-new furniture, this is the only option.

I turn the key in the ancient lock and tug on the handle, but the door resists me. With another firm pull, though, it opens, and a cloud of dust hits us both in the face.

While the woman sneezes, I step inside the darkness and reach around for the light switch I know is on the wall. Finally I find it, and a big overhead light comes on, though the housing is completely covered in cobwebs.

"Whoa," the tenant says.

I realize I don't even know her name. Not that it matters.

I step into the room, which probably hasn't seen a visitor in years now. It's filled with my best antiques—a solid teak dresser, a Victorian vanity, even a four-poster bed that was imported from Germany a hundred years ago. It's all immensely valuable, and I wouldn't be here, showing her this, if it wasn't my only option.

"Amazing," she mutters behind me as she follows me in. "What is all this stuff?"

"My collection." I stand up straight and survey everything here. There are at least two dining room tables to choose from, each with four matching chairs. There's an art deco sofa with red upholstery that should work for her living room, as loath as I am to imagine her eating ice cream on it while she watches mindless television. "If you damage anything, you will be fully liable for paying the value. Out of pocket."

She gapes at me. "But these are antiques!"

"Precisely. They are very valuable, and it would be costly to clean or repair any of these pieces."

"Don't you have, like, *regular* furniture?" she grumps. "I don't need anything fancy."

"These are the options. You can have this couch, or no couch."

She opens her mouth like she's going to snap back at me, but then stops and takes a long, deep breath. Then, she offers me a smile.

"Okay. I'll take good care of it, I promise."

Her smile is so wide that it shows off both rows of her teeth. Her eyes squeeze closed, pinching her rounded cheeks. It catches me utterly and completely off guard.

I should say something, but I find all the words have dried up in my mouth. I nod instead, trying to remember what on earth we were doing here in the first place.

"So do I just pick stuff out, or...?" The woman slides between two end tables, then sits down on the red sofa. "And how do we get it upstairs?"

Oh, right. There's that.

Without answering, I walk around the edge of the room to the big garage door currently blocked off by bookshelves. I scoot one to the side, mindful of the feet, and then reach for the rope that opens and closes the door.

"Select the items you'd like to have, and I will call a friend to come carry them upstairs." I know just who to ask.

The woman's eyes get bigger, and that smile returns. "Wow, really? I can choose anything?" She stands up and surveys the entire space. Picking her way through shelves, she finds a flower-patterned armchair from 1965 and sits down on it, sending up a puff of dust.

I really should have all this stuff covered. Surely Rick will have some plastic sheeting.

"I'll take this," she says, rubbing the soft arm of the chair. Then she continues, clearing away cobwebs that get in her face. She pauses at a small breakfast table that dates back to the eighteenth century. "And this, too. With the two chairs."

I just imagine her setting a wet glass of water on the ancient table and shudder all over.

"I will also give you coasters," I add with a grumble.

I should have furnished the damned apartment myself. I would have used the most inexpensive items possible.

Live and learn, I suppose.

But I do find that I'm enjoying watching her explore my collection. She stops to appreciate all sorts of things—the elaborate engraving on the back of a dining room chair, a soft, velvet cushion on a sofa, the surprising shape of my grand piano. She sits on the bench but thankfully doesn't open the fallboard, only pretending to play over the top of it instead.

Finally, she selects the red sofa, a low table to be used as a coffee table, a desk, and the breakfast set.

"That should be enough," she says, wiping her hands together. "Wow. I can't wait!"

I didn't think this would get her quite so excited. I can only hope she takes good care of my collectibles in the meantime.

"Please note that you are monetarily liable for anything damaged during your stay," I tell her in a stern tone.

She just smiles back at me. "You said that already."

While she enjoys sitting on her new couch, I grumble and head out the door, bound for the hardware store. When I spot my friend Rick in the window, he waves me in.

"I need your help," I say. "Something that'll make good use of all those muscles of yours."

He winks. "Sure thing."

I explain about my new tenant, and he's shocked that I'll be giving her use of items from my collection. Unfortunately, I have no choice.

When Rick follows me inside, the woman gets to her feet and holds out her hand to him.

"I'm Maisie," she says cheerily. He stares at her for a moment, rolls his eyes without answering, and starts picking up the sofa. She attempts to help, but he grunts in annoyance and waves her off, because it's "easier to do myself."

There's a good reason we are friends—both of us are independent and self-reliant. Other people can't be depended upon, anyway.

Maisie and I both wait until all the furniture is carried up the stairs, then I close the garage door. We stand on the sidewalk together, not speaking, until I let out a sigh.

"Anything else you need, *Maisie*?" I can't disguise the impatience in my tone, and the smile falls from her face.

"Oh. Nothing, I guess. Just the Wi-Fi password."

I supply it, the name of one of my favorite Anne Hadron heroines, and then return to my bookstore without saying goodbye.

Thank goodness I can be done with this. Hopefully she doesn't need anything else from me for the rest of her stay.

I really do not like how that smile of hers made me feel.

Maisie

It's too bad the man who runs the bookstore dislikes me so much. I'd really hoped my new landlord could help me get my bearings here, but that won't be the case.

It was rather surprising when he returned from his quest with a minotaur to carry all my new findings up to the apartment. I've never seen a minotaur in person, and the sheer size and volume of him boggled my mind.

But I keep puzzling over Barnaby, the one apparent human in a mostly monster town. Is he just a regular human guy with a truly terrible attitude?

Though I'm exhausted from driving all day, I can't rest while furniture sits in the middle of the living room, so I push each piece around until I find an arrangement I like. I place the sofa across from the television, the chair adjacent to it, with the little table with two chairs in the nook between the living room and the kitchen. It's a tight fit, and all this gorgeous, mismatching furniture looks wildly out of place in the whitewashed apartment, but I like it.

Now that I'm sweating up a storm, I hop in the shower, which has mediocre water pressure and pretty ugly tile. Someone remodeled this place once upon a time, maybe only a few years ago, but they had very old-fashioned taste.

Finally I'm clean and dry, and after massaging some mousse through my hair, I head off to find dinner. From my window, I see a few storefronts that look like they could have food, so I slide on a pair of walking shoes and go hunting.

The diner is cute, though I'd say the mashed potatoes are a little undercooked. The waitress is a faun—I think?—with a uniform on top and furry legs from the waist down, wearing a name tag that says "Lerana." Lerana is sweet to me as she takes my order, and there's a slow-moving, small-town vibe about the diner that's charming. I'm so used to the city, where everyone's always going at a hectic pace and every restaurant is full of people. Tonight, though, there are only three other occupied tables, and my food is delivered within a few minutes.

Maybe I could get used to this. It's not like I go out and enjoy the nightlife back home. I rarely leave the house except to get coffee, and then I spend the rest of the time in front of my computer doing what I love most.

I suppose I can do the same thing here just as well, without the chaos.

While I drink my ice water and finish my dinner, I puzzle over what comes next. What will I do with myself for four whole weeks if I can't work on *Swords of Malroth?*

Maybe I could go back to the game I started building a few years ago. I don't have much in the way of art skills, so I'd started creating it as a pure text RPG.

Hmm. Maybe that's what I should do. Take this moment of respite to work on something for myself and myself alone. I'll need a little inspiration to get back into it, but I think I can manage that.

I head back to my apartment, feeling excited for the first time about this "vacation." Maybe it's the perfect chance to do something that would fuel me creatively. I'd thought about getting into writing or directing once upon a time, but it was just easier to get a job as a programmer.

Curiously, the light is still on inside Barnaby's shop. BOOKSTORE is all that's written across the window. I peer in on my way past, but there's no one visible inside, so I go look at the store hours.

NOON TO 10 PM. Wow. Ten at night? I've never seen a brick-and-mortar business with hours like those.

I'm torn between going inside and heading back up to my room. I don't want to invite another confrontation with the grumpy landlord, but maybe getting back into reading is just the thing I need to find the spark.

Besides, it'll be a few hours before I'm even remotely ready for sleep, even after the long day I've had. My body is too accustomed to going to bed at two a.m.

Cautiously I push open the door to the bookstore, and the bells jingle overhead. I hear a groan from a back room.

"I'll be right there," Barnaby calls.

"That's okay!" I yell back. "I'm just browsing."

There comes another distinctive *harrumph*, but no one emerges.

Good. I can look around in peace for a while.

I scan the titles displayed in front of the counter, where there's a hand-written sign that reads "Recommendations." On the shelf is a history of metalworking, a biography of a long-dead scientist, and some historical novels by Anne Hadron. I've always suspected those books were a little highbrow for me as a girl who grew up reading sci-fi and fantasy, but maybe if I pick one up I can get an insight into the odd man who runs the bookstore. The Anne Hadron looks the least tedious of the bunch, so I choose one at random and put it on the counter.

Then I'm off again searching for what I really want, and eventually I find the fiction section. There's a cover with a pair of swords on it and swooping lettering for the title, so I grab it and add it to my pile.

"Okay!" I call out again. "I'm ready."

Grumbling follows, and a chair squeaks as it moves in the back room. Then Barnaby appears, and he doesn't look all that pleased to see me.

"Hi!" I offer brightly. I'm going to kill this man with kindness. I'm going to murder him with it, until he can't help but like me, at least a little. I need this to work between us for the next four weeks. "Can I buy these two books, please?"

I made sure to put the Anne Hadron on top, and he quirks an eyebrow at it.

"Have you read her before?" he asks.

"Yeah," I answer reflexively, then cringe at myself. I just didn't want him to think I was stupid. "But not much," I add quickly. "This was on my TBR."

Barnaby stares at me with those penetrating, dark eyes of his. "Your *what*?"

"TBR. You know. To be read? The pile of books next to your bed that you always say you're going to read but probably never get around to?"

His lip curls in disgust. "I take a book off the shelf when I plan to read it, and when it's finished, I put it back," he says as the cash register dings. "That will be thirty-two dollars."

I pull out a credit card to pay, and with another sigh, he slides it through an ancient card terminal, and types in the total. After a few moments of awkward silence, it prints out a tiny receipt that I sign with a rather fancy-looking pen.

"Please do not take the pen when you go," Barnaby says, as if people have tried to steal it before. After signing the receipt, I intentionally leave the dark red pen lying on top. He gently slides my books into a paper bag and hands it to me. The front of the bag also just says "BOOKSTORE." I want to ask him what his store is really called, but I don't want to sound like an idiot, so I thank him and head for the door.

"Thank you for your business," Barnaby says as I open it. "I hope... you enjoy Anne's book. That one is my favorite, I think."

I pause halfway out into the street.

"That's good to know," I say. "I'll make sure to talk to you about it when I'm finished."

He's silent, his face unreadable, and the pause drags on so long that I think our conversation might be over.

But just when I'm about to exit again, he says, "All right. I had a lot of thoughts about the ending."

I flash him a sincere smile. "I look forward to it."

Chapter Four

Barnaby

THERE'S A TINGLING IN the tips of my fingers as I close up shop that night—which really just requires sweeping the floor and turning off the lights. I wonder whether the girl upstairs, Maisie, will actually read the book I sold her. She'd also chosen one of those *romantasy* novels, one of the few I carry simply to satisfy the fantasy enthusiasts, and I think she may have just been humoring me by buying an Anne Hadron.

Not that I care much either way. Not that I particularly want to see her again, either, when she smells like something I want to attack and devour.

It isn't a quick walk from the bookstore to my home, but I enjoy the journey, nonetheless. Sometimes in the winter I'll drive the distance so I don't have to trudge through the snow, but I try to go on foot whenever possible, simply to enjoy the wildness of this place.

I follow my usual path through town, where I take a right at the park and continue into the trees. There, the footpath is no longer paved, and I maintain it with gravel so it doesn't get too muddy.

The moon is out tonight, a perfect crescent, without a single cloud in the sky. I still marvel at the pure darkness of the night sky here, and the effervescent brightness of the stars. This is exactly the thing I needed after today—fresh air, with no humans for miles.

I have a new selection chosen for reading tonight, and I'm excited to get back and begin. It's an acquisition that I found online, a first edition of *Dragons, Witches, and Other Paranormal Oddities* from 1858, complete with illustrations. It's always interesting to me to see how my kind is portrayed throughout time, as inaccurate as it usually is.

The one benefit of the internet.

On my walk, though, I find myself thinking less about the book waiting for me and more about my curious new tenant. She made surprisingly good choices when she selected furniture from the back room—all items I might have picked myself. She was so curious and fascinated by what was on offer, and through her eyes, I saw it in a new light. I do have a marvelous assortment, and perhaps I shouldn't let it collect so much dust.

Soon, the manse appears over the tops of the trees. I am home. Smoke is already curling in plumes from the smokestack, which means Adeline has done her job, though she's likely gone home for the night.

Sure enough, when I enter through the front door, the house is a perfect temperature: sixty-five degrees, thanks to the central air Adeline convinced me to have installed. As requested, a fire crackles in the library.

I open the fridge, fish out one of the many milk bottles labeled with my name, and pop open the lid. Cold blood is one of many things I've simply gotten used to over time. I once tried heating it, but the texture became unbearable. It churns my stomach as I start sipping the dark red liquid, trying to keep the bile down as I slurp. It doesn't even stir the monster, to drink such a grotesque thing as mere cow's blood.

I imagine an innocent human like Maisie witnessing that transformation, and the idea of her horrified reaction makes me feel even sicker.

Once I'm as satisfied as I possibly can be with my beverage, I rinse out the glass and add it to the pile to be taken back to the butcher's and refilled.

Then, at last, it's off to the library. My new book is still wrapped, so I peel open the paper to reveal the treasure inside. The cover has clearly seen many hands over time, and shipping has not done the book any favors, either. I will be leaving a chastising review about that.

Once I've opened to the first page, I lower myself into my favorite chair, a high-backed Queen Anne with deep purple upholstery. The fire lights the pages so I can read. Before long, I'm lost in my book, immensely amused by the innocent marvel with which the narrator writes about his discovery of the world's more frightening monsters.

We hid in the shadows for many centuries, many *millennia*, before this book was written. But Anton Cautière began the process of cutting open our identities and revealing us to the world. He writes with such incredulity that I cannot help but feel it, too.

We are marvels, us creatures of the darkness. I'm glad he appreciates that.

It's past midnight when I come across the chapter that Cautière has labeled, "The Fanged Mystery," written in a swooping font.

Here I am. My moment to shine.

Raptly, I read Cautière's story of his first meeting with a vampire. Clearly his subject thought him little more than a humorous annoyance, as the vampire "attack" he describes does not indicate that his attacker utilized his true form. I'm rather disappointed to find that even in these pages, within this first-hand account, there is no mention at all of how fearsome we really are—what we truly hide underneath.

Still, the story leaves the reader with a healthy fear of this "creature of the night." That is, perhaps, my favorite of all mortal misconceptions. Daylight does not hurt us; it simply makes me tired and grumpy.

I wonder if I knew this vampire who encountered Cautière. He could be an offshoot of my old coven when it dissolved. The 1800s were a tumultuous time, and so many of us were lost by the end of the nineteenth century.

It's another two hours before I put the book away and head downstairs. Adeline has kindly cleaned my sleeping room, putting the lid back on my coffin. It was the one they attempted to bury me in when they believed me dead after my own attack. I've since fitted it with silk padding, though the original wood remains.

Before I fall asleep, I think of the stranger's bouncy orange hair, like the setting sun.

Maisie

I return to the diner again the next morning to grab a bite to eat, though I'll need to go grocery shopping today and get familiarized with the kitchenette. I could very well open the cupboards and find nary a pot or pan inside, given there wasn't even any furniture in the apartment when I arrived.

I make a list of necessities on my phone while I eat, and it's disconcerting not being able to text message or check my email on the go. What a weird place. I probably wouldn't have come here if I'd known there wouldn't be *cell service.*

Then again, maybe it'll be good for me. They always say screens rot your brain or whatever, not that I've ever believed it. But is there really a downside to spending more of my time outdoors? From what I gathered, thanks to the map on the counter in Barnaby's bookstore, there are tons of trails around town, and even more the farther you go up the mountain.

After grabbing my groceries, I head back to the apartment to rifle through the kitchen. Sure enough, there aren't even forks or spoons. Every single drawer and cupboard is empty.

Fuck. I'm going to have to talk to Barnaby again, and he's not going to be happy with what I'm asking.

I trudge down the stairs and walk around to the bookstore again, cringing when the front doorbells ring. This time, Barnaby is sitting behind the counter perched on a stool. He's impeccably dressed in a gray collared shirt and a black vest, which shows off the taper from his broad shoulders to his slim hips. The only color on him is the blood-red tie.

I've never found an older man attractive before, but here we are. Damn.

"Finish that Hadron book already?" Barnaby asks, not even looking up from his book.

"Um, no." I stand in the doorway, twisting one foot in my nervousness. "Look, there's nothing up there. No spoons or pans or plates or anything."

Does this man not even eat?

His chest rises with a deep sigh, and finally he lifts his head.

"Did the listing say that it came with those things?"

"I mean, no, it didn't. But it has a kitchen that I can't use."

He snaps the book closed and rises from his stool. "I don't see how that's my problem."

All right, he's not hot at all anymore. He's actually irritating as hell.

But then I remember my plan: absolutely obliterate him with kindness. I won't fall into the trap of making my new temporary landlord hate me.

"Please?" I say instead. "Then the next tenant won't have this problem. Just a few forks, a pan, some bowls—that's all I'm asking for."

Barnaby levels that dark, penetrating gaze on me again, and it feels like one of those dreams where you're naked in school even though you don't remember showing up that way. He studies me for a long time in silence, and I bite my lip to keep from apologizing and backing off my request.

"Fine," he says at last. "If I give you two hundred dollars, can you stock the kitchen to *suit your needs?*" This final part comes out sounding like I'm a spoiled child.

I smile broadly and clasp my hands together. "That would be great."

With a grunt, he fishes out his wallet and opens it to reveal dozens of bills. Dozens of *hundred-dollar bills.* Removing two of them, he hands them to me and puts the wallet away again.

"Is that all?" he asks, reopening his book and sitting down once more.

"Oh, um... yes. That's all." I pause in the doorway. "Thank you."

He doesn't acknowledge me as I leave. Once I'm outside, though, I gasp for air.

That was awkward. Hopefully this is the last time I'll have to ask him for anything, because I don't know if I can stand not telling him exactly what I think of him.

Still, as I walk into the apartment a few hours later with bags full of new kitchen supplies, I have to marvel at the collection of furniture here. I wonder where Barnaby acquired all of this—and most of all, I want to know what it was doing hidden in a dark back room filled with cobwebs.

Barnaby is a mystery, and like every bug I've ever come across, I want to know what's inside.

Barnaby

I wish I knew more about curses so I could cast one on Mayor Louise for convincing me to become a landlord.

The new tenant came in demanding some other thing petty humans need to survive: pans and forks, which I suppose makes sense. Offering these amenities will help me rent the apartment to other vacationers in the future, and what I learn from her could be valuable in making the process as painless and impersonal as possible next time.

If there is a next time. This has all been a rather obnoxious ordeal—especially with the way she *smells*. It's difficult to keep my fangs retracted, to stop my mouth from salivating.

I'd noticed many more things about her on her way out of the store: how her wide hips sashayed and showed off her backside despite her baggy shorts, how her breasts had tugged at the constraints of her T-shirt and cardigan.

Why she was wearing so much in the summer, I couldn't guess, but the appealing shape of her body was perfectly visible despite it.

Perhaps she was sent to torture me. It's been nearly a hundred years since my last taste of human blood, and I thought I had tamed the need inside me with the cow's blood. Well, that clearly isn't true.

But the lust? Perhaps my hunger was simply waiting for the perfect physical specimen to appear. It's been too long, and my instincts are no longer satisfied with such measly nutrition as cow's blood, so my body is responding to that need. Maisie simply appeared at the right time, and her form appeals to me on a baser level.

When I'm home that night, though, I can't stop playing back those moments we spent together. She had such a sweet, wide smile that it felt strange and alien to me. And yet, somehow, it was marvelously appealing. Her lips are just the right size, and in such a lovely bow shape. Her eyes were bright and sparkling, untainted by the centuries.

Even as I lie in my coffin in the early hours of the morning, I can't stop thinking about her. Finally, grumbling with annoyance, I reach down and bring out my cock.

It's just been too long since I had any kind of physical contact with another, that's all. Paired with her scent, it's natural my brain would react to her so strongly. I try to remember this as I carefully stroke myself, maintaining an even pressure from root to tip, but it's impossible for my imagination not to jump back to this afternoon.

When I begrudgingly meet my climax, it's abrupt and powerful. I groan as I spend myself, rocked by how high I went, and how almost painful it was to finish. I'm left panting, my fangs fully exposed, as I fantasize about how such sweet blood might taste.

This arrangement with the human woman is going to be difficult, I can already tell.

Chapter Five

Maisie

I DECIDE TO TAKE my new pact with myself seriously and go for a walk the following day. I drive up the mountain until I reach a turnoff, where there's a parking lot for a nature hike. I've put on my best walking shoes and a worn tank top so I don't fry alive, even though generally I hate putting my shoulders on display.

It's absolutely beautiful up here, I have to admit, and I lose myself in the fresh, bright scent of the trees and vegetation. Huge boulders jut out of the ground, guiding the path up the mountainside. There's some elevation, which means by the time I reach the first twist in the trail, I'm out of breath.

Wow. It's really been too long since I got some decent exercise.

Instead of chickening out, I take it as a challenge: get fit enough that this won't wind me. I've never made time for myself or my body with working on *Swords of Malroth* as much as I do, but maybe now is the time to rectify that.

I work my way up the mountain until I reach the top of the very short peak. There are far higher summits nearby, but I'm gratified to gaze down at the tops of the trees and the small, cozy town spread out below me. Even the water glitters like emeralds.

Then I spot something that wasn't on the map. Off to the south, on the other side of the cove, there's a rather large mansion on expansive wooded grounds. I can't make out the details from this far away, and most of the house is hidden by the trees, but it stirs my curiosity. I wonder who lives there.

At the top of the mountain, I pull out my new book and start reading. It's a typical fantasy, and I lose myself in it for an hour or so before I realize I'd better get going back before the sun goes down. It's an even longer hike down, which doesn't make sense from a physics perspective, but it sure feels like it to my worn-out body. I make it to town just in time for the quaint streetlights along Main Street to turn on, casting an orange glow on the wide sidewalks. Only one or two cars putter down the road, but otherwise the street is quiet.

The bookstore, though, appears to be open. I've bothered Barnaby enough for today, so I should really go back to my apartment and get started making dinner. Still, I pause outside and watch through the window as he rearranges the books on a shelf near the counter, then stands up straight and adjusts his vest again.

When he bends over, I lean closer. Holy fuck, that man has an *ass* on him. It's tight and muscular, and his gray slacks highlight the curves of it beautifully.

I back away from the window, but it's too late. Barnaby has turned around and caught me staring directly at him. He rolls his eyes, and I'm about to flee when he waves me in.

Wait, what? He wants me to come inside?

Cautiously, I open the door and step through.

"No point standing around gawking," he says when I come in. My shame at getting caught is surely turning my face pink. "Did you get everything you needed?"

I nod rapidly. "Yes, the kitchen is all stocked up now."

He nods, but when I look into his eyes, I find his pupils huge and black. Maybe he has a vision problem, and that's why he keeps the lights low in here.

"You're out late," he remarks. "Past sundown in a monster town? Very bold."

I realize belatedly that I didn't even consider it. "Should I be afraid?"

To my vast surprise, Barnaby chuckles. I didn't know he was capable of laughing.

"No, there's nothing to fear here. But maybe stay inside the town limits after dark. Monsters may not be a problem, but bears and cougars are."

"Oh. Right." I didn't consider that when I was out hiking. Maybe I should take bear spray with me next time.

Then I remember I mowed through half of my book today up on the mountain, and I should probably get another one. I used to love to read as a kid but lost the desire when I started using computers at school. I knew right away that the computer was where my destiny lay, and it became the object of my full attention.

"Do you have the sequel to the one I bought last time?" I ask, moseying over to the fantasy section. Barnaby arches a brow.

"*Ash, Bone and Diamonds*?" He joins me in front of the rack, then points it out. "That one."

I pick up the book with a similar cover, but blue instead of red. Then I head to the checkout, and he meets me there.

Barnaby seems significantly less surly today, and I wonder if perhaps he woke up on the wrong side of the bed the first time I met him.

"Your store's open pretty late," I say, noting that it's nearly closing time. "Why's that?"

"People read at night," is his only answer as he rings me up. I pull out my card again, pay for the book, but stop him as he's about to bag it up.

"It's fine. I'm just carrying it up the stairs." He passes me the book and a receipt. "Thank you."

"Try the Hadron," he says as I head for the door. I pause and peer at him over my shoulder. "It might surprise you."

"I definitely will."

Then he smiles. And holy shit, is it an incredibly sexy smile. But then I notice his long canines—much, much too long. Supernaturally long, and curved at the tips.

"Whoa." The word comes out before I can stop it. Maybe he isn't so human, after all. "Are you... a vampire?"

Barnaby's eyes widen, and then he covers his mouth, muttering something I can't hear under his breath. He puts even more space between us, heading behind the counter.

"Yes." It's a single, factual word. "Goodnight, Maisie."

He won't look at me, and his brows are knit tightly together. I know when I'm being dismissed.

"Goodnight, Barnaby," I say quietly. Then I head back to my apartment, wishing I hadn't said anything at all.

Barnaby

Well, there's one cat out of the bag. Not much I can do about it now.

The way Maisie's eyes went wide, she must be afraid of me. I think back to the Cautière book, and I'm glad that most mortals don't know about our true forms. Then she might really have gone running for the hills.

But she smelled so absolutely lovely, fantastically divine. That's the only reason I smiled at her, and it was a mistake.

I grumble to myself as I close up shop for the night and head home. I don't need that sort of temptation around, not when I've gone this long avoiding it.

That's why I founded Hallow's Cove, after all—so I wouldn't have to face this. Most of the year, the humans stay away from our town. In the winter, they're all up at the lodge on Twilight Peak, so I don't have to interact with them much. It's only in the summer when it becomes a problem, but no one has ever smelled as powerfully delicious as Maisie.

Why did she have to be *my* tenant?

My whole walk home, I'm thinking about that pulsing vein in her throat, the one letting off that incredible aroma. Simply remembering it and I'm getting hard under my slacks.

Has it really been so long since I drank blood?

I know that I'm a disturbed individual. Living for 230 years will do that to you. I've seen many things in my life that would turn most mortals' stomachs, as horrendous as history has been. Even now, in the thick of rapidly advancing technology, I watch the corruption that still rules over the world, merely changing form over time from one type of dictator to the next. The invention of the cell phone may be the worst of them, taking the place of books in people's minds, closing them off to all the marvelous lessons that history has to offer.

Now the world's mistakes will repeat on an even shorter timeline.

Not that I'm absolved of guilt; I've made my own errors, committed my own atrocities. I will own those. I cannot pretend the years I spent with the coven didn't happen, as much as I wish now that they hadn't.

After my glass of chilled cow's blood, I settle into my chair beside the fire and pick up my book just as I did last night, and the night before that, and every night since I built this mansion beside a bay that few others had ever seen.

When I'm finished with Cautière's chapter on werewolves, I make my way once again into the basement where Adeline has prepared my coffin.

I will not see the human woman any more than necessary for the next four weeks. And then she will be gone, a memory in the wind like every other tourist in my town. I can't risk waking my true form, not after so much time. I don't know that I have the capacity anymore to control it, and that would be the worst thing that could happen.

Maisie

It is a lovely town, I'll give Hallow's Cove that. Main Street has all sorts of attractions, from the adorable little flower shop to the boutique that carries cute, summery dresses and boots. I'm still getting paid while I'm on this forced vacation, so I consider buying something to wear in case I see Barnaby again.

I wish I hadn't reacted to his fangs the way I did. Surely it seemed like I was afraid of him, when in truth, I was just surprised. It makes sense that he would be a monster, too, in a place like Hallow's Cove.

I finish my book that night, unable to sleep. I'm not used to running a normal schedule like this, when my body typically doesn't get tired until two or three in the morning. Eventually I give up and head over to the computer to work on my pet project.

It's almost three when I realize I should be asleep if I don't want to waste tomorrow. But it takes me forever to drift off, thinking about Barnaby's smile, fangs and all.

I'm exhausted the next day, and I pledge to find some way to cure my insomnia and return to a normal schedule. Maybe when the investigation is over and I can go back to work, my boss will appreciate me working nine-to-five like everyone else.

Once again, I go on a hike, finding a different trailhead this time, and work on my new goal of becoming fit. Once again, I run out of breath partway up, but I keep trucking. By the time this vacation is over, I'll be a machine.

I carefully avoid the bookstore when I get back to the apartment, and this time, I order a burger from the diner for takeout. It's when my hands are all covered in grease that I realize I didn't think to buy napkins or paper towels.

There's a drawer in the wide base of the table, so I open it delicately with my pinkie and see if perhaps a stray dining napkin has found its way there. Sure enough, I discover some embroidered blue napkins, and hastily wipe off my greasy fingers.

Hmm. If there are still napkins in this table from when it was used who knows how many years ago, I wonder what else might be stashed away?

The bottom drawers of the dresser, which I didn't end up needing, contain what appear to be ancient bed sheets. There's a very old copy of a Dickens book in the nightstand, and in the desk drawer are some pens and yellowed sheafs of paper. I wonder how old this desk is.

Curious, I flip them over and find lettering on the other side.

Dearest Barnaby,

Has it really been two years since we were at the Foster gathering together? Time has slowed to a crawl since then as I wonder about your fate. Perhaps you eloped after I saw you leaving with that woman, or worse, perhaps you have died and this is a pointless endeavor. I would very much like to know which it is. If it is the former, I will celebrate for you, and if it is the latter, I want the opportunity to mourn you properly.

I have sent this letter to our mutual friend in the hope that he will pass it along to you. Perhaps you have simply chosen not to speak to me again after some slight I cannot remember. In that case, please allow me to apologize, for I would very much like to see you again.

Your beloved sister,

Beatrice

I read the letter again, knowing I'm doing something I shouldn't. The moment I found this, I ought to have put it back in the desk and pretended I never saw it. It's none of my business, and it feels rather personal. Barnaby must have forgotten he left it here.

What very much startles me is the date at the bottom: May 24, 1842.

Oh, wow. This letter is nearly two hundred years old. I drop it onto the desk immediately, running to wash my hands with soap and water. I hope I haven't gotten any grease on a piece of memorabilia like that.

I wonder if Barnaby even knows it's here. What if he's been looking for it for decades, and it was inside this desk all along?

It's late, nearly closing time for the bookstore, but I pick it up and march down the stairs anyway, determined to give it back to him. And perhaps, if I'm lucky, find out about this sister of his.

Did she ever find him again?

Chapter Six

Barnaby

Tourist season is in full swing now, so there are two people in the store browsing when the bells jingle and a familiar scent wafts in.

Damn. It's Maisie again, clutching something in her hand. What does she want this time? I thought I'd gotten rid of her.

"All right," I call out to the older couple browsing the non-fiction. "Closing time."

They grumble but choose something anyway—two matching sudoku books. As they check out, Maisie stands patiently in line behind them, her eyes focused on me. I wonder what she wants now.

Finally, they exit the store with a jangle of bells, and she steps up to the counter. I lean forward on it, propping my head up on one hand to pretend I'm disinterested. The smell of her is even more acute every time I see her, and now my own blood starts to heat the closer she gets to me.

I need her to leave.

Maisie begins with an uncertain tone. "So, I found something in... one of the desk drawers."

She glances away from me and then back again, and I wonder what she's discovered that would make her so uneasy. I suppose I haven't looked through my furniture in decades, and it's certainly possible I left something behind. The desk used to be mine, once upon a time, but I didn't think I'd left anything of significance in it.

"What is it?" I ask in a bored tone. Shifting from one foot to the other, Maisie slides a piece of parchment paper across the counter.

I blink down at what is certainly my sister's handwriting. I snatch the letter up, quickly scanning the words, dreading what Maisie might have learned from reading it.

I shouldn't care. Her opinion of me doesn't matter. We don't know each other. She's a tourist passing through, like all the others. But when I reach the end, the last words I ever heard from Beatrice, my heart constricts.

How I had wanted to write back. How I wanted to find her at the address she'd written on the envelope. My only sister, who shared my mother's womb with me, who came into the world mere minutes after I did.

We never saw each other again after that cold, winter night, and I will forever ache in a place that cannot be soothed, even by the passage of time.

I whip the letter off the counter and tuck it under the cash register.

"Thank you," is all I say, because my head is swimming with thoughts. This is the story of how I changed, how I became what I am, and all the things I left behind afterwards.

And Maisie has now read it.

She cocks her head. "Your sister? Did you ever write back to her?"

I scoff. "Is that any of your business?"

Maisie falters, her hands falling back to her sides. "I guess not." She turns her head away. "I just thought it might be important to you. That's all."

I hate how she appears as if I've sucked all the air out of her. She may be just a tourist, but we will have to tolerate each other for many more weeks as landlord and tenant, so perhaps I should be kinder to her.

"It is a sore spot," I finally admit. "This is from the very beginning of my second life."

"Second life?"

I don't answer as I rise from my stool, then walk to the front door to flip my OPEN sign to CLOSED. I shut the door, lock it, and turn off the front light before padding back to my seat. Maisie watches me the whole time like a hawk.

Why has she taken such an interest in my history?

I beckon for her to follow, and hastily she does, walking with light footsteps as I head toward my reading room at the back of the store.

"My second life as a vampire," I begin, opening the door and leading her inside. Among the priceless texts tucked away on the shelves, we sit down in the two matching armchairs. "There was no way I could write back to her, after that. I was different. Changed."

Maisie leans forward, rapt. "So you didn't see her again? Not ever?"

As much as it pained me at the time to ignore Beatrice's letter, I couldn't be in her life from then on. I would only bring her heartache, and at such a young stage in my vampirehood, I had very little control over my need for blood. The worst thing that could happen would be to attack my own beloved twin sister and feed on her. No, there was another, even worse option: if I turned her, too, and sentenced her to the same endless life of hunger that I lived.

Though I have mastered my cravings over time, still it lingers, still it aches—especially now, in Maisie's presence, with her scent filling up the reading room.

It was a bad idea to bring her back here.

I shake my head. "The best thing I could do for Beatrice was to cut off all ties with her. To let her believe I was dead. That was the kinder act, really."

But Maisie looks devastated. "I can't believe it. Your own sister." Before she drops her eyes to her lap, I see red veins forming in the whites, and they are growing shiny. "That's terrible. I'm so sorry."

Sorry? I squint at her. She is a stranger to me, and yet she's shedding tears over something that does not concern her at all?

"I have had more than a century to get past it," I say, hoping to assuage her remorse. There's certainly no need to cry about it. "I am not bothered anymore."

This isn't entirely true. I have simply learned how to lock Beatrice away into a box in the back of my mind and leave it there.

"I have a brother, too," she says abruptly. She wipes her face with one wrist, scattering the tears. "He's younger than I am by a few years. If I thought he had died, if I never heard from him again... I think that would be one of the most painful things possible." She tilts her head. "You couldn't have at least written her back? Assured her that you were alive?"

I huff at her interrogation. "It would have been giving her a false hope. I *did* die that day, Maisie." I use her name to drive it home. "The man who was Barnaby Hallow died, and I am what took his place."

"Wow." Her voice is hushed. "But you are still him. You loved your sister and you still do, don't you?"

Of course I do. She was the most important person in the world to me while I was still alive. Women in my life came and went, and our parents eventually passed away. At the end of it all, Beatrice was there, always by my side.

"I don't see how this conversation benefits anyone," I say harshly. "She died. It's over. It cannot be changed now. How I feel about her to this day is of no relevance."

Maisie furrows her brow. "Sure it is. That's a lot of grief that you haven't really worked through, it seems like."

"Is this that 'therapy' I am always hearing about?" I snap. "Do you have a license?"

She looks surprised at my outburst. "No? But grief is normal, Barnaby. We all experience it. And sometimes we ignore it, rather than truly feeling it. And then it grows bigger and bigger inside you until it's suffocating you."

I bark a laugh. "I am not being suffocated. The opposite. I am free because I have divorced myself from my mortal life. You know nothing about my past, my history, my—"

"I'd like to," she says, so quietly I almost can't hear her, and I stop abruptly.

Disbelief colors my voice as I ask, "Why?"

She tilts her head and smiles sadly. "You're interesting to me. Now that I've seen this, I want to know all about you. You've lived so long and seen so much..." She glances up at the ancient leather-bound books lining the shelves. "You're like one of these books, but flesh and blood."

"So I am a curiosity to you? A character in one of your little fantasy novels?" The words are biting, though I'm not sure why I am attacking her this way. I understand the need to know more, to learn more about a history I was not present for. The quest for knowledge is the most honorable one there is, but the subject of Maisie's fascination is painful for me.

She shrugs. "Is that so bad? I know I don't have much to offer as a *mere mortal*," she says the words with a dripping sarcasm that surprises me, "but I would like to know more about you. Maybe we could be friends?"

I balk. *Friends?* I have two acquaintances that could be, potentially, called "friends"—Rick, who only moved here recently but also despises triteness, and Harley, the owner and bartender at Killy's Bar. I do not befriend tourists, who will come and go and never return. It's a pointless effort.

"No, we cannot be friends," I say. Maisie's brows jump in surprise. "You are my tenant, nothing more."

"Why?" she asks right away. "What's so wrong with me?"

"You will leave, too!" I don't realize I've raised my voice to such a boom until Maisie flinches. "What is the point? Why should I grow attached to someone who will only leave?" I rise from my chair. "I think it's time for you to go now."

I expect this to have hurt her, but instead she's studying me intently.

"Just because something doesn't last doesn't mean it's not worthwhile," Maisie says, also getting to her feet, but she doesn't move to leave. "There's so much you can learn, even from a passing moment."

I shake my head, even while a deeper part of me latches onto her words. Could there still be value in knowing a mortal for just a few weeks? Is there something to be gained from being *friends* for such a short window of time?

"I'd like to talk again soon," Maisie says while I stand there, silent as a fool. "Would that be okay? I really am curious to learn more about your life. If you're not offended by it."

I can't fathom her fascination with me. Just seeing Beatrice's letter tonight has already reopened so many old wounds.

And yet... it is complimentary, too. Someone is interested in the many years I've passed on earth, most of which feel meaningless to me now. Would it really be so bad to pull back the veil on time?

But there is so much I can't tell her. The coven must remain hidden, for I cannot bear to face what an innocent like Maisie would think of its existence—or of the things I did as a member. But perhaps I can fill her head with other oddities, other experiences.

I sniff the air, and her smell has grown more intense. That is the other important question: can I really bear to spend more time this near to her? It's stirring something fearsome inside me, breathing in her aroma, and yet I'm luxuriating in it. I would very much like to repeat this, even as it pains me not to simply leap on her and bury my fangs in her throat.

"Fine." I grind out the words despite myself. "We can meet again, if you want it so much."

Maisie's face brightens. "I mean, I have nothing to do here, and I don't know anybody. I think this is the perfect thing while I wait for some corporate asshole to decide my fate."

I don't know what she means by this, but it stirs my curiosity.

When the woman leaves, I lock the door behind her. Hopefully my centuries of self-control will keep me firm and steadfast. That I will not reveal my true self.

I do not drink from humans. I never will, not ever again.

Chapter Seven

Maisie

BARNABY'S MOOD SHIFTS LIKE the wind, which somehow makes him all the more fascinating. I want to know what's going on inside his head that makes him so capricious, angry one moment and then thoughtful and introspective the next.

I have an idea of how long he's been alive, given the letter. If I'm right about his age, he was probably born around the turn of the nineteenth century. After starting his "second life," he lived through world wars, massive global shifts in power, and who knows what else. I'm infinitely curious what it was like.

The invention of the phone. Radio. Television. Internet. It's all happened in his lifetime.

And of course, there's the part I'm less willing to acknowledge, that he is a fine specimen of a man. Even when Barnaby scowls, there's a rigid set to his strong jaw and a tension in his broad, sharp shoulders that appeals to me. Strength is coiled up in there along with mystery, and I want to unravel it. I want to soothe those shoulders, to dig into the layers of him and find out what he's hiding underneath it all.

The next day, I'm bouncing on my toes, excited for this new turn my forced vacation has taken. I've been reading to keep myself occupied in the meantime, and today I'm going on another long hike despite the ache in my calves. I need a better pair of boots, so the first thing I do is head to the outdoor store down the block.

The shoes cost a pretty penny, but it's worth it when I get up the mountain and have no new blisters on my feet. Again, I sit on a big rock overlooking town, pull out my book, and read until my limbs are stiff and I need to head back down.

I return to the bookstore in the late afternoon, just as the sun is beating us with its warmest rays. It's a Sunday, and the town is quiet. There are no customers in the bookstore when I arrive, so hopefully that means Barnaby will have plenty of time for me.

Why do I want his undivided attention so much?

He's intriguing to me, that's all. Besides, I have nothing else to do here in Hallow's Cove besides hike, read, and work on my project at night while I should be sleeping.

The bells jingle overhead as I enter the shop. Barnaby isn't behind the counter, but he soon appears behind a rack of books. I'm surprised when my stomach does a flip.

"Hi," I call out nervously, waving a hand.

He sets down a stack of books he was restocking and approaches me, and I realize then that he's usually sitting down, so I wasn't aware of just how tall he is. I have to tilt my head back to look into his face. It's set in a stern expression, as usual, and this time, his nose is crinkled up.

Do I smell bad? I suppose I didn't shower after hiking, though I think my deodorant is still working.

"We'll sit out here," Barnaby says. "In case... customers come in." He stalks to his reading room in the back and soon emerges with another stool, which he plops down on the other side of the counter, then gestures for me to use it. Happily I sit down.

"I always thought vampires had to hide in the daytime," I say, gesturing out the window at the bright summer day. "It doesn't bother you?"

Barnaby gives me a blank look. "Where did you hear that?" He laughs outright. "Humans will spread the strangest rumors. I don't particularly enjoy direct sun—it makes me tired and irritable—so I tend to stay inside in the summer. Perhaps that's where such a silly myth started. I'm not the only vampire who finds it exhausting."

I wonder how many other false things I've learned about his kind. Is everything I thought I knew just a stupid rumor?

"How did you turn?" I ask. The letter had mentioned a woman taking Barnaby away at a party, and a twinge of jealousy tickled at the back of my neck when I read it.

Did that woman bite him? How long did he stay with her?

With a deep sigh, Barnaby turns his dark gaze on me. "Are you sure that's a story you want to hear? It is a dark one."

"Yes, of course!" I want to know everything. "If it's not too painful for you."

Barnaby sighs. "It was a long time ago. It is less painful and more *cumbersome*."

I glance up at the clock. "Well, I stay up late, so I have all the time in the world if you do."

"All right. I must confess that I don't have anywhere else to be." He turns away again. "It began when I went to a gathering with friends of ours—mine and Beatrice's. We were living in Vienna at the time, and there had been rumors of people disappearing off the streets." He shakes his head and sighs. "I wish I had listened. I wish I had been more cautious after the fourth newspaper article about someone going missing in the middle of the night."

"A vampire?"

He shoots me a look that clearly says, *don't interrupt me,* so I snap my jaw closed. I know I'm lucky that he's agreed to do this, and I shouldn't push it.

"Not just one. An entire coven had taken up residence in the city, I would later learn. It was the leader of that coven, Eleanor, who found me at the party that night."

Barnaby's eyes wander away from me to focus on some point on the wall, and I don't think he's looking at it so much as remembering something that happened long ago. His brows crease as he digs up ancient memories.

I don't interrupt this time, and eventually he speaks again.

"It was a rainy night, so everyone was drinking something warm. A lovely woman arrived at the party late, and though I asked around about her, no one knew who she was. But she had a confident air about her, a sort of dark humor, and it drew me to her right away."

Another unexpected tingle of jealousy. I try to tamp it down as I listen to his story.

"We talked for ages that night, into the late hours. She had lived a marvelous life, though she looked barely out of her twenties. She'd traveled all over and had many stories to share. I was entranced. Enthralled."

I grit my teeth, knowing what's coming.

"I was so monumentally foolish not to see the signs," he says, shaking his head in disappointment. "There was no way she had done and seen so much in her short life, but I accepted it all anyway. I didn't question her too-long teeth. When she invited me to leave the gathering with her... I agreed."

His eyes close and he pauses for a time, as if dredging up this point in the story hurts him. I wonder if I've made a mistake by asking for this. I didn't want to inflict pain.

"I'd had so much to drink, I didn't even notice when she led me deeper into the city, toward the district known for being... what is the word now?" He puzzles over it for a moment. "Sketchy?"

I have to laugh. "Yes, that's the one."

"It was not safe, but I wasn't paying attention, too excited at the idea of what Eleanor had in store for me. I had not engaged in, er, relations in a few years, and so I was eager."

My jealousy grows bigger and toothier, imagining Barnaby having *relations* with this woman. Still, I ask in a breathless voice, "What happened next?"

He gets that faraway look in his dark eyes again. "She took me inside an old abandoned building, and I figured that she had an apartment upstairs. I was so trusting. Once inside, I was immediately surrounded, and the ritual began."

"The ritual?" I echo, sounding kind of like an idiot even to my own ears.

Barnaby just nods, lost as he is in his memories.

"She had chosen me. Eleanor was the leader of a coven, and they were trying to grow. Every member selected their own victim—and I was hers. I would be her apprentice, she told me. That's probably the last thing I remember before she attacked."

I'm starting to regret asking him for his story when it's clear by the curl of his lean body and the strained look on his face that this was a terrible moment.

"She almost completely drained me," he says, his voice quieter now. "Left just enough blood in my veins to keep me alive. Then she began to feed me *her* blood. By then, I was so desperate to live that I accepted it. I gladly put my mouth to her wrist and—"

A choking sound cuts him off. I thought this man didn't have these kinds of emotions, but clearly, I'd been wrong. I'm tempted to hop over this countertop and put an arm around him, though I don't think he'd welcome that.

"That was it," he says suddenly, sitting upright. His eyes are darker than before, and now, a pair of very sharp, very white canines have protruded from his mouth. Something about the intensity of that memory must have triggered him. "From then on, I was like her. A vampire. A creature. Her *servant*."

I can't mistake the venom in his voice. I wonder what happened to Eleanor. Did he kill her to get away?

"But you're free of her now?" I ask, hopeful that he'll tell me the next part of the story.

Barnaby gives a sharp nod, his eyes focused intently on mine. "She is a memory, like all the other memories. One worth forgetting." He pauses, swallows harshly, and then continues. "I came here not long after, intent on getting as far away from people as possible. I was... a danger back then."

I don't miss how he glosses over his time with Eleanor, how he doesn't tell me the way he left her.

"And then, somehow, all of this happened." He gestures around us. "One day I had a plot of land in the middle of nowhere, and the next day, other monsters began arriving who had heard of me, wanting a place they could rest and recover, and, sometimes, hide. We didn't allow humans here back then—but times always change."

So that's how Hallow's Cove came to be. It's a refuge for the inhuman, for those who needed safety. I feel like an intruder here when this history is much deeper than I could have imagined.

"Where'd you get the name?" I finally ask, trying to bring the mood back up after his painful confession. "Hallow's Cove?"

Barnaby squints at me like I have two heads.

"Well, it's my name. Barnaby Hallow."

I feel like the biggest dumbass that ever dumbassed. I glance down at the counter, where a clearly-visible plaque reads "Barnaby Hallow."

"Maybe if I'd used my eyes," I joke, picking it up. "Sorry. Just not very observant."

He quirks a brow. "But you found this, didn't you?" he says, holding up the letter that he's hidden under the old-fashioned cash register.

I shrug. "Sometimes I get lucky."

The double entendre seems to occur to both of us at the same time, and I snort while Barnaby looks away, his cheeks darkening.

"Can't be that lucky if you ended up here on vacation for an entire month," Barnaby says with a scathing chuckle. "There isn't a month's worth of things to do here for a human."

"If I do get lucky, I'll go home sooner."

He cocks his head. "Oh? How?"

"If the investigation concludes that I'm not at fault for what happened." I'm admitting that I'm responsible for a huge fuckup and not even really on *vacation*, after all. But after what Barnaby just told me, I think it's all right to give him the truth. Maybe then he'll come to trust me, and let me in on the rest of his story.

His eyes widen. "Investigation?"

I take a deep breath, and then dive into my tale. When I finish explaining how Wade demanded that I go on paid leave, Barnaby is unabashedly staring at me.

"You had to be *forced* to take a vacation?"

I shrug. "I love my job. It's all I've ever wanted to do. It's my whole life." I didn't realize how much it hurt to be accused of making such a disastrous mistake, but it aches to think I've failed at the one thing that gives me joy.

"So that is why you're always up at night," he says, tapping his chin.

I nod. "I've always been a night owl. That's why this job is so important to me—I love the work, and the hours are the only reason I'm still sane."

He offers the slightest smile, and it's the first one I've ever seen. "A fellow denizen of the darkness," Barnaby says with a snicker. "You would make a good vampire."

I'm surprised by the tingle I feel all over at this compliment. I don't think he doles them out often.

The bell jingles as the door to the shop opens, and a big family walks in, introducing a wild explosion of sound to the otherwise silent bookstore. Barnaby cringes. I step away from the counter as he rises to his feet and asks them, "How can I help you?"

I take this as my cue to leave, as much as I would enjoy sitting and talking even more. He has a business to run, after all.

But as I head for the door, I hear Barnaby call, "Maisie!" I turn around, and he abandons his salesman role to come over to me. "I would... like to hear more about your work. Perhaps late some evening, when we are both more in our natural habitats."

My heart takes off into a thundering roar. "I would love that."

He offers me another one of those tiny smiles, then returns with a roll of his eyes to helping the family choose new picture books for their children.

When I'm back in my apartment, I spend the rest of the evening trying to read, but I end up thinking only about Barnaby's story. There's much he left out, that was clear. What did he do after he was turned? What became of Eleanor?

I wonder what it would take to learn everything.

Chapter Eight

Barnaby

THAT HUMAN WOMAN IS much more appealing than she has any right to be. I found her annoying at first with her pestering questions and sunny demeanor, but I understand much more about her now. She is devoted to her work and derives most of her life's pleasure from it. Having it ripped away from her has clearly taken its toll, though she tries to hide it.

I can understand such a thing. I have always been a bookseller, and my joy is sharing my passion for the written word and recorded knowledge with those who seek it. Decades with the coven stole that from me—just one more reason that they were the darkest years of my time on this earth.

Sitting in such close proximity with Maisie's scent, though, was nearly torture. All I wanted was to sink my fangs into that throbbing vein in her throat. And yet I invited her to spend even more time together, to sip on her sweet smell even longer, though it will be painful not to drink from her.

I am a glutton for punishment, it seems.

It is only a few hours later that I step out the front door and lock up the shop behind me.

"Hi."

I whirl at the sound of Maisie's voice. She's sitting on the step leading up to her apartment and gives me a tiny wave.

"Have you been waiting for me?" I ask.

She bobs her head. "I just felt like there was so much more I wanted to ask you. If you're amenable to doing it tonight."

I swallow hard. I thought perhaps I'd have an evening to recover from how delicious she smelled earlier today, but I have no reason to turn her down.

"I will need to go home and feed soon," I hedge, "but I am available for another hour or two."

Her smile lights up her face in a way that's surprisingly appealing. Her teeth aren't perfectly straight or perfectly white—they're very average in both senses, which I find adorable.

"Great. Do you want to come up for a drink?"

I give her a deadpan look. "Unless the drink on offer is your blood, I think I will decline."

A laugh bursts out of her, and though she stifles it with her hand, she still can't hold in a final snort of amusement.

"All right, all right, I won't offer you a beer, then, if you come up."

That wasn't how I expected her to react to the threat of being fed upon, but I'm pleased by the result. She doesn't find me frightening, and that gratifies me.

"I will come upstairs," I say.

With a grin, she opens the door to her apartment and ushers me in behind her, as if I don't own the place myself. I follow her up the stairs, unable to look away from the sweet sashay of her hips as she leads me to the top.

Underneath those baggy clothes, I wonder what she really looks like.

"I'm going to have a drink," she says, "but please, take a seat." She even pulls out a chair for me at the small table before she heads to the fridge and pulls out a glass bottle.

When we're seated across from each other again, she uses a bottle opener she must have purchased with the money I gave her and leans forward on the table.

"So what happened after you were turned?" she asks. "You didn't tell me that part."

"I thought we were here to talk about *your* life." The last thing I want is to tell her all the terrible details of that time. I did many, many things I'm not proud of, and I would very much like to forget those years myself.

She squints. "Hmm." After taking a long drink of her beer, Maisie sighs and leans forward on one hand. "Not much to tell. I have pretty normal parents. Still married, still embarrassing. I also have a little brother finishing up his master's degree."

It sounds as if she has a normal family, which explains some of her emotional steadfastness.

"I wasn't a cool kid growing up because I loved the computer too much. Played a lot of video games, and started trying to make my own when I was in middle school."

"Middle school? And you were creating games of your own?"

She laughs. "Well, I *tried* to make games of my own. It wasn't always successful. I only managed to make a bad version of Snake before I took a class at the local college in high school." She rubs her hands together eagerly. "That was really where it started. I started making changes to the games I liked, so I could play, uh…"

She trails off, her eyes darting away from mine.

Now I'm curious. "So you could play…?"

Maisie blows out an irritated breath, scattering a lock of her curly hair. "I wanted to see the character naked, okay?" She turns her head away. "So, I installed a mod that made everybody in the whole game naked."

I can't help a laugh, and it feels somewhat rusty rolling off my tongue. She altered an entire video game to fuel her perversions.

It's incredibly charming.

"What?" Maisie blows her cheeks out, affronted. "I was in high school. What do you expect?"

"No, no." Another laugh tumbles out of me. "I'm not making fun of you. It is a wonderfully genius idea for an adolescent."

She snorts into her hand. "I love when you use words like that. *Adolescent.*" She drinks more of her beer. "Well, it wasn't that genius, because eventually I got caught playing it on the school computers. That was the beginning, and now, here I am." The happiness on her face fades. "Potentially without a job, depending on how this investigation turns out."

I don't like that her sweet demeanor has disappeared. I much prefer it when she's smiling and telling a story.

"How did you get your current job?" I ask instead, guiding us back onto a safe path.

"Well, I knew this guy, Wade. We'd met once before, actually, on a dating app."

I'm surprised by a twinge of envy. Of course Maisie has dated on one of these *apps*. She is a fine young woman in the modern age, and certainly too young for someone like me, even if I were still mortal.

"Anyway, Wade and I weren't compatible at all"—this instantly soothes me— "but he did help me find this job. Now he's my boss, which in this case, wasn't so good." She sighs into her palm. "I feel like I disappointed him, as my friend and my supervisor, and that's the worst part."

I can understand this sentiment. It's one thing to make a mistake that only affects yourself, but to make life harder for those you care about?

It's the reason I left the letter where it was. The last thing I ever want to think about is how I disappointed Beatrice—how she lived her life and grew old thinking I was dead, and by the time I saw her obituary in the paper, it was far too late to ever mend the bridge again.

Maisie

I've bared my soul to Barnaby, and now he sits across from me, looking pensive.

"If this investigation concludes that it was not your mistake, you can go home?" he asks.

"Yep. But if they find it was a mistake on my part..." I don't want to think about the worst possible outcome. "Maybe a pay cut. A demotion." I shiver. "Which I don't mind. As long as I get to keep my job."

Quite suddenly, tears bubble up behind my eyes. Maybe it's just the beer, but the reality feels too close.

"I can't do anything else," I say, rubbing my face with my fists to keep it at bay. "I don't *want* to do anything else. I love my work. I love watching videos of players playing my game and having fun. I can't lose that!"

Unable to hold it back anymore, I drop my head into my arms to hide my crying. I don't know what Barnaby's expression looks like, and I don't want to know. He's probably embarrassed at me bawling my eyes out over nothing.

I hear footsteps, and then a gentle hand lands on my shoulder. My head shoots up.

"From everything you've told me," Barnaby says in a quiet voice, "you are good at what you do. I'm sure they will find you innocent."

His kind words only make me cry harder. I don't know how long this has been building up, but now that I'm letting it out, it's coming like a flood. I turn in my chair to look up at him as tears stream down my cheeks.

"Th-thank you. I j-just…" I can't even get the words out.

Barnaby crouches down next to my chair, and before I can react, he slips his arms around me. My body goes still as he brings me in close, pressing my cheek to his chest.

He smells incredible. He's both hard and soft under me, and his calm, easy breathing immediately calms me. His big hand strokes my back as I shake with another sob.

"It will be all right," he murmurs, speaking into my hair. "You won't be stuck here forever."

I want to object, to tell him that since I met him, I don't feel *stuck* here. But at this stoic man's tenderness, at his sympathy and affection, I fall apart, and my words escape me.

I cry like that into his chest while he rubs circles on my back. Finally, when my tears start to dry up, Barnaby releases me—but he remains there, kneeling by my chair as I sit up and try to regain my composure. While I sniffle, he reaches out and pushes a stray curl of hair away from my face.

"Thank you," I mumble, rubbing my eyes now that they're all scratchy and dry. "I didn't realize how much I needed a hug."

Barnaby's lip quirks into something that could be a smile. "I'm glad to have helped."

Why are his lips so… appealing? As if he can read my mind, he flicks his pink tongue out and licks them, and I'm drawn to it like a fucking magnet. Our faces are already so close together, it wouldn't take much to lean forward and—

I don't realize I'm already tilting my chin up toward Barnaby's until he tips his head down closer to me, too. Is he thinking what I'm thinking? Oh, I hope so.

Yes. I think he's about to kiss me.

When our lips meet, it's quiet and gentle, just a light press of skin on skin. But the intimacy of it, this sudden crossing of the high barrier between us, nearly blows me over.

Instantly my body is on fire, and all I want is *more*. This tiny taste of his lips has ignited something bigger, so tentatively, I press harder with my mouth. Barnaby returns my pressure easily, quickly, with even more force.

Fuck. Even without tongue, his kiss is wonderful. He works expertly over me, caressing my lower lip first, and then my top one. His hand lands on my cheek, guiding my head even closer to his, pushing us more firmly together. I whimper against him, this surprising and delightful touch more than welcome in my sad state. To be seen as attractive, to be understood, to be heard and felt, almost pulls more tears from my eyes. I raise my arms and wind them around Barnaby's neck, falling further into him as our kiss deepens.

And then his tongue strokes my lip, and a moan escapes me as my mouth opens for him. But he doesn't rush—no, a man like this doesn't invade right away. He simply explores, testing me, creeping in and then darting back out again in an invigorating, tantalizing tease. I could just melt into a puddle as his other arm loops around my back to anchor me, his hand sliding from my cheek to the nape of my neck to deepen our kiss.

When his tongue slips between my lips at last, everything inside me clenches. Somehow this simple kiss has become monstrously erotic in mere moments. It's easy to picture how Barnaby would feel without his starchy vest under my hands, how his arms would caress my bare skin. I sag in my chair, putting all my weight on him, and he gladly takes it as our tongues twine together, lips wet and no longer tentative. I can barely breathe with how ferociously Barnaby is gobbling me up, his hand applying even more pressure to the back of my head as he pulls me off the chair and fully into his arms.

Finally, I have to come up for air. When I open my eyes, I find that his are huge and dark, his pupil filling his entire iris. There's an odd glow in them, something that's distinctly inhuman, as I slide fully into his lap on the floor.

"Maisie," Barnaby murmurs, his voice suddenly quite deep, almost ethereal. "You smell so damnably good."

I blink. I *smell* good?

Before I can ask, he hauls me up to my feet. Immediately I'm set off-balance as he wraps me up in his arms once more, his whole tall body bending down to meet me for another deep, enthralling kiss.

I'm drowning in the most exquisite way possible, and I think it would be fine if I met my end here, swallowed up by Barnaby Hallow.

Barnaby

Hell, I shouldn't be doing this. I shouldn't be here, in my tenant's apartment, kissing her until her lips are swollen and her cheeks are pink. I shouldn't be getting closer to this woman who smells so divine, whose pulsing veins make me hungry in more ways than one. Touching her body this way, my hands trailing up and down her sides and sliding over the curve of her hips, is treading on dangerous ground. I'm already imagining touching her this way without clothing between us, and I'm getting hard as a rock under my slacks, all while my fangs protrude from my gums.

Maisie tempts me. She invigorates me. She's drawing up a part of my soul that I thought had long gone dormant—the part of me that craves pleasures of the flesh as much as it craves blood. It's been a hundred years since I kissed a woman, not to mention slept with one. It's too risky to be intimate with a human when it brings my true form so close to the surface. I feel it lurking just underneath, salivating at the scent of Maisie, imagining sliding inside her while my fangs sink into her throat.

And yet I can't find the willpower to pull away. I'm a victim of my need, unable to stop what's already been set in motion. My hands creep under the hem of her shirt, encircling her waist, the pads of my fingers sampling the softness of her bare skin. Of their own accord, my hips press into her, though I am much taller. Likely she can feel my carnal desire against her belly—and yet Maisie doesn't object. No, she's tumbling even deeper into my arms, willingly giving herself over to the demands my mouth and hands are making of her.

I suckle her lips, teasing them with my fangs, and she lets out another sweet whimper as my fingers caress her body. Her own hands skate down my shoulders to my waist, and to my surprise, she pulls me even tighter against her.

So my erection is both noticeable and welcome. This fills me with a nearly overpowering heat, knowing that she's attracted to me, that she's as turned on by me as I am by her. She is young and virile, soft and pliant, and oh so very human.

Human. She is merely mortal. She is a woman but she is also prey, and the monster is surging closer and closer to my consciousness.

If I don't stop now, it may reveal itself, and then I will never get to taste her again.

At last, at the terrible image of Maisie's face when she sees my true form, I regain control of myself. I pull away from our kiss hastily, seizing her by the shoulders and shoving her back a step. Maisie lets out a squeak of surprise as I force a solid foot of distance between us. We're both panting, chests heaving, and electricity crackles everywhere we're touching.

"I'm sorry." I drop my hands and take yet another step away. "I'm so sorry, Maisie."

She blinks, confusion in her eyes, which are still red from her tears earlier.

"Sorry? For what?" She tries to return to me, but I keep my arms up, shielding myself. Her brows furrow, and her mouth tilts down. "What happened?"

"Nothing." I turn from her and stalk toward the stairway that will lead me out of her apartment.

"Barnaby?" When I glance back, her lip is trembling, and the shakiness of her voice nearly breaks me. "Where are you going? What did I do?"

She thinks she has done something wrong. At the very least, I must assuage that.

"You didn't do anything." My voice comes out deeper, harsher than I intend, because the need to feed is so strong. "I made a mistake."

"A mistake?" Tears gather on her lashes again. "But... you..."

"I know. And I'm sorry." It feels idiotic to be apologizing again, especially when I don't regret kissing her at all.

No, what I regret is that I ever became a vampire. That I ever left that party with Eleanor. That I allowed myself to be tricked like a newborn calf and doomed myself to this life where my desire can never be gratified—where I would cause fresh weeping in a beautiful woman.

But I leave her there anyway, fleeing down the steps to the sound of her crying.

Chapter Nine

Maisie

WHAT DID I DO wrong?

Everything was going so well. Better than "well." I hadn't realized how much I wanted Barnaby until I had him, and then it took over completely.

And he wanted me, too. That much was clear in the way he kissed me, how his boner had not-so-gently nudged at my stomach. That had sent ripple after ripple of desire straight from my throat to my crotch, imagining what he might do with it.

But then... something happened, and I wish I knew what. Did I move too quickly? Did I offend him somehow?

I collapse on the couch, which I realize now smells of Barnaby, too, and cry harder.

I'm such a whiny fucking baby.

Finally, I wind down to a few miserable sniffles, getting snot all over my wrist when I try to wipe my face. When I peer at myself in the bathroom mirror, I find my eyes puffy from crying and my lips swollen from how fiercely Barnaby kissed me.

Of course he ran. My face is beet red and my hair is wildly mussed. I look like a train wreck.

Pledging to myself that I won't cry again, I brush my teeth, dress in my pajamas, and climb into bed, feeling like the shit on the bottom of someone's shoe.

I'm never going to be able to look him in the eye again.

The next morning, I lie in bed for hours, watching the sun rise and pass overhead through the window. Eventually I get up because my stomach is roaring for food, so I pull some orange juice out of the fridge and smash a grocery store muffin. Then I sink down into one of my chairs, the same one where I sat last night when Barnaby kissed me.

I groan and drop my forehead to the table. What a mess. I kissed my landlord, like a fucking idiot, and I still have to deal with him.

After moping, I drag myself out of the apartment and carefully avoid the bookstore. I don't have the energy to go on a hike, and the air is even hotter today than it was yesterday. Instead, I meander down Main Street, stepping into the flower shop to smell the sweet aroma of the plants, browsing the boutique—anything I can do to keep my mind off what happened last night, and how Barnaby ran from my apartment like his feet were on fire.

I rack my brains trying to figure out what I did wrong, what misstep I took, that interrupted what had been so fiery and wonderful between us only a moment before.

And then, I start to feel angry.

He couldn't have at least held a conversation with me? He'd simply apologized over and over, then left. Wasn't I owed at least some explanation?

When I head back home after having a rather pathetic solo dinner at the diner, I stop in front of the bookstore. I'm still sad, yes, but now I'm pissed off, too.

And I want Barnaby to know it.

He's inside the shop, holding a book but not reading it. He appears to be staring at the wall and doesn't even notice me standing there. Then, as if he can feel my eyes on him, his head abruptly turns to look at me.

His eyes widen, and a frown pulls down the sides of his thin mouth. He doesn't wave or usher me in. We simply stare at each other through the glass, and my anger rises higher and higher as he does nothing.

Feeling ferocious and clawed, I flip him the bird.

The second I do it, I turn around and sprint back to my apartment. I slam the door behind me and run up the stairs as fast as I can, wondering what came over me.

I just flipped off Barnaby Hallow, a two-hundred-year-old vampire, because he didn't want to make out with me.

God, I'm such an idiot.

Barnaby

I continue staring out the window long after she's gone, dumbfounded.

Fuck you.

That's what the look on her face said, even if her hand hadn't done the trick.

But it was a good thing I'd left when I did last night. I'd raced around to the back of the shop, my fangs protruding from my lips, my cock aching. There, hidden from the apartment upstairs, I finally gave in and let my true form take over.

I hate the way my bones creak as it stretches me, as they seize and grow inside my skin. It's always painful to become him, to turn into the monster that isn't in any of the history books.

Because people who see it never live to tell the tale.

Eight feet tall and equipped with massive wings, I took off into the air, still fully erect from the memory of Maisie's lips. I didn't get far before I was forced to handle it, and beating my wings high above the cove, I stroked my cock over and over before easily meeting my finish.

It felt like a lewd, disgusting act, thinking of her while I did it—like a violation. But it also felt so, so good, and a release I desperately needed after how hungry Maisie had made me.

That night, reading next to my fire brought me no pleasure. I abandoned it early to retreat to my coffin, where I spent many hours remembering the sound of Maisie's little whimpers and moans as I kissed her and touched her all over.

I expected not to see her the next day, and now I wish I had never gone up to her apartment. I'd come to enjoy her company, but I doubt she will grace me with it again.

Maisie flipping me off through the store window was the last thing I expected after I left her in tears. She is sweet and full of emotions, but apparently she can be vicious, too.

I suppose that anger is better than sadness. Perhaps it will sustain her until she receives the results of the investigation and can finally go home.

Tomorrow the shop will be closed, so I'll have no reason to come near her. Besides, I need to return my bottles to the butcher, Beau, and pick up a fresh batch of cow's blood. Perhaps it's like drinking pond water, but it sustains me, and that's the best I can ask for in this world.

I go to bed fantasizing about what Maisie's blood would taste like and how her soft body would feel underneath me.

My two days away from the bookstore drag past. Adeline visits to tidy and dust, as she does every other day. Together we restock the firewood, because heavy lifting is much easier for me than it is for her. That is the singular benefit of my true form, I suppose—it grants me abilities such as these even when I'm human.

As I sit at the kitchen island drinking some especially fetid-tasting blood, Adeline pauses in the doorway. Though she is older than I am by a hundred years, she still looks to be in her mid-thirties, with long hair that she keeps pulled back in a tight bun. Even when she comes to my home to clean, she wears very little in the way of clothes, as many creatures of the forest are wont to do.

"Something is different about you today," Adeline says, arching one eyebrow. "What's changed?"

I frown. "Nothing has changed."

She surveys me critically, and I don't think she believes me for even a moment. How does she know about Maisie? Nymphs are insightful and can sometimes even leech emotions from those near them, but surely I've hidden my bubbling feelings better than that.

"Mr. Hallow." Adeline sits down at the stool on the other side of the island from me. "I have served you for nearly fifty years, and I've never sensed trepidation in you as I am sensing it now."

Fucking wood nymphs.

"It's personal," I say, more snappishly than I intend, so I sigh and shake my head. "Apologies, Adeline. But I have found myself in a strange situation, and I don't know if I'm enough of a man anymore to navigate it."

She cocks her head. "You are fully a man still, Mr. Hallow, so I'm not sure what you mean."

I sigh as I rub my temples. I know Adeline well now, and she will not let this rest until I tell her the truth.

"There is... a woman," I say, forcing the words out, "who has moved into the apartment above the bookstore."

Adeline nods, encouraging me to continue.

"I made the mistake of growing closer with her. I believe we share an affection for one another."

When I fall silent, she leans forward. "And? I fail to see the problem if she returns your feelings."

"That is the problem," I snarl. "You know what hides inside me, Adeline. You know about the monster that could emerge. I would harm her. I would want to drink from her. And you know she would flee, screaming, if she saw it."

I have shown my true form to my housekeeper once in the past, and even though she is supernatural, too, it surprised her.

"You don't know that," Adeline says. "You're making decisions based on assumptions."

"No." I shake my head firmly. "She is an average human mortal. And I don't know what the creature would do to her."

"The creature is you, Mr. Hallow." She rises from her stool. "It's not separate. You have spent many mortal lifetimes honing your control. I doubt that you would hurt her."

"How can you possibly assure me of that?" I snap, unable to hide my irritation. If it were so easy, I wouldn't be in this predicament.

"I can't assure you of anything, of course." She shrugs as if this is a moot point. "But if you truly share an affection with her, perhaps you should let her at least make the choice for herself, rather than making it for her. It's not fair to you or to her to deny yourself every pleasure. You deserve happiness, too."

But I don't. Not after what I did with the coven. I will never deserve happiness after the misery I wrought on others.

"Thank you for your advice," I say in a clipped voice. Adeline sighs and nods, understanding that the conversation is over, and leaves the room to finish her chores.

What *would* Maisie do if she saw my true form? I don't know if I could bear her running away screaming.

But what if she didn't?

Chapter Ten

Maisie

THE NEXT DAY, THE bookstore is closed, much to my relief. I don't have to avoid it just to keep from seeing him.

I'm tired of moping around. I need to recover this vacation somehow and start over—without Barnaby Hallow on the menu.

Feeling determined, I go on a long hike and find my stamina has already improved quite a lot. I make sure to stretch plenty, and my new boots are holding up well. This time, when I reach the squat little peak at the top of the very first hike I did, I'm barely winded. Feeling emboldened by this small success and driven by my fury at Barnaby, I continue on to the next peak.

It's a difficult trek, and I meet some scree along the trail that makes the way especially treacherous, but I relish the challenge. Making my muscles burn has me feeling strong and powerful. It hurts now, but I'll emerge on the other side a much better hiker for it. Maybe by the time

I'm ready to leave, I could even attempt the highest peak in my tourist brochure, which would take me all the way up to the ski resort and even past it. It's a seven-mile hike to get to the top of Twilight Peak, while all I can manage right now is two miles each way.

That's when I decide that will be my goal. I'm going to get to the top of this damned mountain and scream. I'm going to conquer this place before I go home. No matter what happens with the investigation, if I can reach that point high up in the sky, I'll know that I accomplished something during my time here.

When I reach my destination for today, I pull out the fantasy book I've nearly finished. Great. I'm going to have to go back to the bookstore, or crack open that Anne Hadron novel I bought, as boring as it sounds.

After reading for a while under the beating sun, I shove everything back into my pack, sling it over my shoulder, and head down the mountain again. The scree is even more challenging going this direction, but I can tell I'm developing new muscles I never even knew existed. Maybe I'll go home with ripped legs and a great ass.

When I'm finally back on flat ground, my calf muscles are shot, and I hobble to my car. I stop at the diner on my way and absolutely devour a chicken-fried steak with extra gravy, then I order a piece of cream pie on top of it. I feel like I could eat an entire cow myself.

When I reach the apartment after the streetlights have come on, the bookstore is still closed, dark, and locked up.

Something aches in my chest. I'm trying to stay mad about what happened with Barnaby to cope with how rejected I feel, but deep down, I'm sad, too. I wish I knew what happened so I could have tried to fix it. I wish we could have talked it out instead of Barnaby running from me.

I don't like how lonely I feel walking up the stairs by myself, knowing I have no one in this town to even call a friend anymore. Perhaps I should try a little harder. Maybe with some outgoing, extrovert energy I could make friends with the sweet faun who works at the diner, or one of the two wolven behind the counter at the coffee shop.

And there's always the bar, too. I'm not much of a drinker—just a beer here and there—but alcohol makes great social lubricant, and it might embolden me enough to approach a stranger.

Instead of going up to my apartment to work on my video game project, I meander down the block to Killy's Bar. Just hovering outside the door, I can tell it's loud inside. The part of me that stays locked up in my apartment most of the day flinches at the idea of going in, but I need to get past that.

I push open the door and step into the noise. The lights are low, and a few people sit at the bar, while others are scattered around at small high-top tables. There are a number of obvious monsters here, from the minotaur, Rick, who helped move my furniture, to a white yeti with blue skin. He's chatting up a little fairy woman with glittery wings. There are a few humans mixed in.

Surely with this variety of people available, I'll find a conversation partner.

I sit down at an open spot at the bar between the fairy woman and a scruffy blond man sipping a beer. He looks like he hasn't shaved in weeks, and there are dark spots under his eyes.

"Would you like something to drink?" The bartender approaches me, drying a glass. She would appear human if it weren't for the actual living snakes on her head, which hiss and move on their own.

"Just a beer. Something light."

She nods and walks away to pour it. The man next to me remains unmoving, not looking up from his drink.

"Do you live here?" I ask him, since the fairy woman is already engaged in conversation with the yeti.

His eyebrow lifts and his eyes flick over to me.

"Just moved here," he grunts.

"Gotcha. I'm on vacation."

He searches me for a moment longer. "Good for you."

"What brought you here?" I ask. He appears to be human, so I wonder how he ended up in Hallow's Cove.

"None of your business." The man turns back to his beer, glowering even more.

"Ooookay," I say, leaning away. So much for making friends. "You don't need to be rude."

The man suddenly spins on his stool, and his very hair is bristling. "And you don't need to be fucking talking to me," he snaps, eyes wild.

I shrink back in my seat, and his outburst has caught the fairy woman's attention.

"What's going on over here?" she says, tilting her head.

"Nothing!" The angry man gets up, and now he's simply shaking with rage. "Everyone needs to mind their fucking business!"

"Whoa now." The yeti gets out of his seat, too, holding his hands up. "Chill out, Jeremy."

"Don't tell me what to do!" the man—Jeremy—roars. "If this *woman* hadn't been prying into my business—"

"Calm down." The yeti puts a hand on Jeremy's shoulder, and the blond man grows even more enraged.

"I'm perfectly calm!" His eyes are blazing.

With a sigh, the yeti grabs him by the arm and tugs him to the entrance to the bar. Jeremy snarls, but some of the fight drains out of him.

"I know this werewolf stuff is all new to you," the yeti says, "but if you can't keep it together, you shouldn't go out."

Werewolf stuff? I wonder. Perhaps that's why he's so out of control.

"I'm doing fine!" Jeremy snarls.

He's clearly not doing fine, but he follows the yeti out the door, anyway, and it falls closed behind them, leaving me gaping at what a mess I just caused.

The fairy woman turns to me with pity. "Don't worry. That's not your fault. That guy... he's new to town and just had some recent, um, *trauma*."

I blink at her. "Oh. That's too bad."

"Not that it excuses what he said to you," she clarifies. "But new werewolves have a hard time at first after they're turned."

A shudder runs down my spine at the thought I might have been in real danger just now. I take a few more sips of my beer before I get up and slap some bills down on the table. I need to get out of here before something else happens.

"You're leaving?" the bartender asks, her snakes all rising on her head to look at me.

"Yeah. Sorry."

I flee the bar as fast as I can. So much for making friends.

My legs are horribly sore when I wake up, so I decide to give myself a day off from hiking. But that means finding something else to do, instead. I try not to mope about the bar event last night and decide I'll give it another shot—maybe somewhere more casual.

By the time I'm finished with my morning coffee, I find the street has been blocked off and vendors are setting up tables along the sidewalks. There's a sign that reads HALLOW'S COVE STREET FAIR hanging between two lampposts.

Hmm. That's convenient. Maybe if I'm friendly and outgoing, I could try again today.

Curious, I look around. The diner is putting out a variety of pies, while the flower shop has vases full of gorgeous, sweet-scented arrangements covering the table. Even the coffee shop is setting up a station to serve pour-over coffee and cold-brew coffee. A stall from the

Hoffman farm has already set out coolers full of fresh milk and eggs, and I browse the adorable displays they're putting out about each of their animals.

Then I spot him: in front of the bookstore—and my apartment—Barnaby is slinging a tablecloth over his table. I can't make out his expression from this far away, but his shoulders are hunched as he unboxes a puzzle and dumps out the pieces.

Making a note to avoid that part of the street fair, I keep walking until I reach the end, and then turn back around.

I'm going to have to go past him if I want to get into my front door, but I'll delay that as long as possible, even if I'm not pleased with my long sleeves in the growing heat. But after I've browsed the entire fair twice, and my hands are sticky from the candy I bought outside the chocolate shop, the sun has risen higher in the sky, and I desperately need to go inside and change.

I watch Barnaby's table until he's occupied with some children, and with his head turned, I sneak around the side. But just as I make it to my front door, and safety, he whips around to look at me. His dark eyes catch mine, and his eyebrows rise high on his forehead.

Quickly I shove my key into the doorknob, but the stupid thing is so ancient that it takes a lot of fiddling. I focus on it, trying to pretend that Barnaby isn't staring at me, but it just won't fit. Damn it. Today, of all days?

"Let me help."

After what happened at the bar last night, the unexpected voice over my shoulder scares the living daylights out of me. I leap back from the door, panting, and find Barnaby standing there with his hands up in surrender.

"I'm sorry," he says. "I didn't mean to startle you."

Moving slowly, like he's trying not to frighten me further, he takes the key in hand and gently wiggles it into the mechanism before turning the knob.

Obediently, the door opens, and I glare at it. So it won't work for me, but it rolls over dead for the vampire?

"Thanks," I grind out, endeavoring not to look at him. No, if I look at him, I might get weak for that stern chin and proud nose, the streaks of gray and the dark eyes, and I don't want Barnaby to know that he hurt me. I don't want him to see on my face just how sad I am and give him the gratification of knowing he caused it. I flipped him the bird, after all, and made it very clear where we stand with each other.

That's the final image I want him to have of me.

I push the door open and step in, then try to kick it closed behind me. But it *thumps* as something stops it.

"Maisie."

I swing around, wondering what's in the way, only to find Barnaby has placed his foot in the door to keep it from closing.

"What are you doing?" I snap. "I could have hurt you!"

"No, you couldn't."

When I don't try to close it again, Barnaby withdraws his shoe from the gap.

"What do you want?" I cross my arms. "Don't you have a booth to run?"

He glances over his shoulder at the table covered in puzzle pieces, where kids are picking through them, then back at me. "Yes. But this is more important."

I scowl, but don't answer. If he's got something to say, he can say it now.

"Maisie, I'm sorry."

I frown even deeper. "You said that already. The other night. I get the picture."

Barnaby pauses and his lips screw up, like he's tasted something bad. "And I'm sorry for that, too. I shouldn't have left without explaining myself to you."

I laugh. "Don't worry. The message was received." I reach for the doorknob again to close the door. "Can I go now? I'm sweating like crazy."

"Not the right message," he says. "Not the one I should have given you."

"What does that mean?" I'm not in the mood for guessing games right now.

"It means..." Barnaby trails off, then swallows hard. He looks away from me, down at the floor, before finally steeling himself. "It means that I'm very attracted to you, Maisie. Too much."

My gaze darts up to his. Those black eyes are focused intently on me.

"You are?" I ask, wondering if I heard him right. Why would he have left the other night if he was actually into me?

"Very much so." His voice drops lower, deeper. "And sometimes... I cannot control my urges. I was afraid of what I might do to you."

As if to demonstrate his point, his sharp white fangs protrude from his lips. He leans closer, and a new prey instinct inside me strongly suggests running away. This is a creature made to kill humans and drink our blood.

But I'm not scared of him. I may not know Barnaby all that well, not yet, but I don't believe he would hurt me even if he lost control.

He's far too stoic for that.

"Bullshit." I grab the door again. "I don't believe that for a second. Now will you let me go?" I want to get away from him because the scent of his cologne is fucking hot. The top two buttons of his shirt are open, probably to increase airflow in this heat, and the skin underneath is wonderfully pale and smooth. I wonder if he looks like that all over.

I shake my head and try once more to close the door. Barnaby doesn't stop me.

"Of course I will let you be," he says, taking a step back. His brows crease. "I just wanted to make sure that you knew that... you're a beautiful woman. An exquisite conversationalist. You have a bright and curious mind."

I hover with the door halfway closed. "That's a lot of compliments."

"I know. And I mean all of them."

I peer at him through the gap, still suspicious. "What are you after? Why did you tell me all this?"

Barnaby straightens his vest. "I'd like to start over and try again, if you would let me."

"Try *what* again?"

He fixes a stern, serious gaze on me. "I would like to try wooing you."

I gape at him. *Wooing me?* Who uses a word like that?

Besides, I'm already wooed. I'm already stupidly attracted to this man, no additional wooing needed. But I don't want him to know how pathetic and needy he makes me feel—not to mention how much the idea of him losing control appeals to me.

What would he do? Would he drink from me? Bury those sharp, dagger-like teeth into my throat and suck on me, just the way I'd like him to suck elsewhere on my body?

I am curious what this *wooing* entails.

"Fine," I finally say, attempting to keep my excitement in check. "What did you have in mind?"

Chapter Eleven

Barnaby

I SHOULD HAVE BEEN a little more prepared for her question, but I hadn't thought it all the way through when I followed her back to her apartment. Still, I manage to come up with something on the fly.

"Come to my home," I say in my gentlest tone. "Only some of my collection resides in the bookstore, but the vast majority of my prize possessions are at my house, in my personal library." I lick one of my fangs surreptitiously. "I believe there are some collectibles there that would pique your interest."

Maisie arches a brow, her arms still crossed over her chest. She is quite pissed off at me, enough that I know it will be a project to dig myself out of the hole I'm in.

"You want me to come check out your home library?" she says, arching an eyebrow.

It does sound rather silly when she puts it like that, but she loves to learn and ask questions, and I think there are many items among my shelves at home that would whet the appetite of her curiosity.

If she's willing to give me another chance, that is.

"Yes. I will serve you a meal, and then perhaps I can show you some of my more valuable treasures?"

She looks skeptical. "A meal? But you don't eat, do you?"

"I can still cook." I'm very much interested in the pink flush that spreads across her pale, freckled cheeks.

"Oh. Okay. Well, then, um…" Her eyes dart away from mine. "I guess that would be fine. When?"

"Tomorrow? After I close up shop?"

What I'm proposing is dangerous, but I have no choice. Not seeing Maisie for a few days was too much for me. As much as her scent makes me crave her, it also makes me desire her company. I enjoy her, truly, and I don't want this ugly energy between us to persist.

"Fine. I'll go to your house."

I can't help the smile that spreads across my face. My cheeks feel stiff at the unfamiliar motion.

"I will see you tomorrow night, then." I tip my head, then turn to glance at the station I've set out for the fair. Grimy children are tossing puzzle pieces at one another, and my hands curl into fists. "Now I must go and take care of this."

Maisie gives me a small, pitying smile. I am happy to see it on her again.

"Go," she says, flapping a hand. "We're on for tomorrow."

With a thankful nod, I turn and storm back over to my station, where I call for the children's parents. Hastily they pick up the thrown puzzle pieces, and I thrust a free bookmark at each of them before urging them to leave.

But tomorrow night, I'll get another chance. I hope I don't ruin it.

The following morning, all the groceries I requested are already on the table when I wake. Adeline took care of them, making sure I would have everything I need tonight to make a fine meal for Maisie.

The last time I cooked was when I was still alive. I did not build this house with the intention of cooking in it, though it does have a modest kitchen and I'm grateful for that now.

All day at the bookstore, I'm consumed with the thought of tonight. I look up recipes, curious at how more modern ingredients might improve the meal I have planned. I'd intended to make root vegetables, game hen and an apple pie, but discovered while researching that better, more modern spices could be introduced to the pie to bring out the apple's natural flavor.

When it comes time to close shop, I find Maisie standing out front waiting for me.

"I don't know where your house is," she says, twisting one of her toes on the ground. "Can I drive behind you?"

"I did not drive," I say. "I walk. But it is a long way, so if you have your car, then we ought to take it." I don't care much for cars, but they are a necessary evil in modern times.

"Oh, okay. Well, I'm in the lot out back. Come on."

She leads me to a vehicle unlike anything I've ever seen before. It's shiny and chrome and looks more like an airplane than a car. There is also no door handle.

"Sorry," Maisie says, hurrying back to the passenger side to help me. She presses a button, and a handle pops out. "Pretty cool, huh?"

I glare down at it. "Unnecessarily complicated."

Her face falls, and I regret it immediately. With a sigh, Maisie returns to the driver's side and we both get in. The seats are black, and there are screens everywhere.

"I thought this was a car," I say. "But it appears to be the interior of a spaceship."

Maisie laughs as she pushes a button and the vehicle turns on. "What about a little bit of both?"

Then she zooms out of the parking lot. I grip the door as she comes to an abrupt stop at the street.

"Where to?"

Encouraging her to go more slowly, I guide Maisie down the darkened streets and deeper into the woods. We hit the dirt road that will take us around the cove, and the undercarriage of her low car grinds as it hits a pothole.

"Not even paved?" she asks, aghast.

I shake my head. "No construction machinery is allowed out this far. It would disturb the wildlife."

"What kind of wildlife?"

"You don't know? Hallow's Cove is home to a rare owl. I worry that overdeveloping the forested areas would damage that habitat."

Again, Maisie is quiet as we drive down the darkened road. She slows down even more, as if she might hit one of those rare owls by accident. Thank goodness.

Finally, the trees around us recede and the manse appears. I show Maisie where to park next to my own vehicle, which is sheltered in a carport. When we get out, she checks the underside of her spaceship for damage. It's clearly precious to her.

As we head inside, though, she pauses in front of my car.

"Really?" she asks, gaping at it. "This must be from the 80s!"

"Indeed. I purchased it new in 1981."

She runs a hand over the faux wood paneling. "A Wagoneer. Wow. Haven't seen one of these in... well, forever, except at car shows."

"It is good for the dirt road," I say by way of explanation. She simply shakes her head in awe.

I urge her to follow me into the house and show her where to deposit her shoes at the door. "Don't worry. Adeline keeps all the floors well swept."

Maisie cocks her head. "Adeline?"

"My housekeeper." I lead her to the kitchen, and her eyes travel over everything—the floors, the walls, the furniture, even the ceiling.

"That's a lovely chandelier," she says. "And the wood grain in this floor is gorgeous."

I'm glad that she appreciates it, as each of these details was a conscious choice when I had the manse built many decades ago.

"Please, sit." I gesture to the table. Obediently Maisie pulls out one of the chairs and makes herself at home. Fetching a glass from a cupboard, I pop the cork of a bottle of wine and pour. When I set the glass in front of Maisie, though, she frowns.

"You didn't have to get me wine. I know you don't drink."

"I told you I would provide for you tonight. Please, allow me?"

Taken aback, she clutches the wine glass tight. "All right." She exhales. "I'll let you."

The way she says it, though, I wonder what other things she might let me do.

Maisie

I am mesmerized by Barnaby as he busies about the kitchen, dicing an onion, then switching to a pan to cook it. The wine he chose is impeccable, despite the fact wine isn't really my thing—but he seems intent on providing me a certain dining experience, and I'm a willing recipient.

I sip as I watch. I don't want to distract him, so I don't make conversation for the first twenty minutes. Eventually, though, Barnaby turns to me and cocks an eyebrow.

"You aren't typically so quiet."

I flush. "Are you saying I don't know how to shut up?"

"Sometimes," he says, but his lip twitches playfully as he turns back to what he's doing.

Did he just make a joke at my expense? I think I like it.

We make light conversation as Barnaby puts something in the oven and sets a timer. When it goes off, he brings over a bowl of salad, a plate of root vegetables soaked in a sweet-smelling sauce, and an entire Cornish hen to the table.

"What on earth?" I ask, gaping at the rather large meal. "I can't eat all this alone."

"Don't worry. Whatever you don't eat, I'll set it aside for Adeline."

I still can't believe he has a housekeeper. Who keeps house for a vampire?

Feeling self-conscious that Barnaby isn't going to join me in eating, I try to be civilized as I slice off a piece of chicken and add it to my plate. He has something in his hand—a tall glass that looks like it's also filled with wine.

"What's that?" I ask.

Protectively, he curls his hand around the glass, as if hiding it from my view. "Cow's blood." There's shame in his voice. "From the local butcher."

So that's how he survives without taking human blood.

"Doesn't look like it tastes very good," I say, observing the sour look on his face.

Barnaby shakes his head. "It truly does not. But it's how things have to be."

I puzzle over this as I continue eating, and a companionable quiet falls. The meal he's made is wonderful and reminds me of meals my mom made on holidays.

"How long has it been since you drank human blood?" I finally ask, breaking the silence.

Barnaby's eyes widen, then they dart away from my face. He furrows his brow as he looks down at the glass of blood.

"That's not a story to tell over dinner," he grumbles.

I get the sense once again that he's hiding something—perhaps from that same period of time he glossed over when he told me his story about being turned. I wonder what it'll take for him to tell me the truth.

"I see." I tilt my head. "What about after dinner?"

Something in Barnaby's expression changes in a way I don't quite understand. His eyes bore into mine, and they're darker than before.

"Perhaps," he says carefully, "we could talk more then."

Barnaby has still not looked away as he sips his blood. I'm much more self-conscious about how I'm eating, and I try to take smaller, cleaner bites. His gaze darts down to my mouth, then back up to my eyes, and a sudden, unanticipated shudder of need runs straight from my throat down to my belly.

Wow. How does he look so fucking sexy with just a *look?*

I thought that was it, but then Barnaby produces a pie from the oven, and it's just as magical as dinner was. Finally, I'm stuffed as full as the Cornish hen I just devoured, and I set my plate and utensils aside. Barnaby collects them, but when I offer to help with the dishes, he rolls his eyes.

"You are a guest. Stay put."

So I remain seated as he clears the plates and washes them by hand, even though there's a dishwasher installed next to him. I get the sense it's never been used.

When he's finished, Barnaby offers me a hand. I'm surprised by the gesture but take it gratefully. He doesn't let me go as he leads me out of the dining room and into the rest of the house.

First, we visit a sitting room, with matching couches and chairs organized around a low table. It doesn't look as if this room is used often. The next one, though, appears much more lived in. A fire is lit in the fireplace, though I don't remember seeing Barnaby light it when we arrived. Deciding to keep my questions to myself for now, I follow him into the softly lit den, where a single chair and ottoman sit next to the fireplace.

What's most marvelous about this room, though, are the bookshelves. They line every wall, and each shelf is packed to the gills with books. Most of them appear to be canvas- or leather-bound—certainly there are no mass market paperbacks among them.

"Wow," I mutter, approaching one of the shelves. I'm about to reach out and pull out a book when a hand lands on mine.

The smell of Barnaby fills me up, and almost on instinct, I lean back into him. He sucks in a sharp breath but doesn't move away as his hand guides mine back to my side. There, he twines his fingers with my own, and it sends an electric shiver up my arm.

"These are some of my most precious treasures," he says into my ear, making the hair on my neck stand on end. "Many are older than I am."

Now I understand. I wonder if they might simply fall apart in my untrained hands. He reaches out with his other arm and plucks a title from the shelf with his long, delicate fingers. Then he opens it in front of me so I can see the pages clearly.

"This is my favorite novel," he says, his voice even quieter now, but closer.

"What sort of story is it?"

"A love story." He shuts the book again and releases my hand, then sets the book gently in my outstretched palm. "Perhaps you would enjoy it."

With that, he walks away, leaving me standing there, now cold from his absence.

Tucking the ancient book carefully under my arm, I follow him to the fireplace. There he sits down in the chair, and I hover next to him, not sure where I should go.

Then he pats his lap. My eyes fly up to his, because certainly he doesn't mean for me to sit there.

"Would you like to read some together?" he asks, but there's a distinctive, seductive lilt to his voice.

"You were going to tell me your story," I say with petulance.

"Hmm. That is a sordid tale, though. I would much rather spend my time with you thinking of... better things."

I have to admit that it appeals to me, too. I want him close to me again, to feel his cool, expert hands on my body.

No. I want to know what he's hiding, what part of his history he's so intent on keeping from me. I want to fully understand him before we move any deeper into this, because I'm certain that it's tied to the reason he left me that night in my apartment.

I sit down on the ottoman instead, and disappointment falls across Barnaby's face.

"Please," I say, settling the book in my lap. "I won't judge you. I just want to know."

He studies me for many long, silent moments, before he finally closes his eyes and sighs.

"Fine. If you insist."

"I do."

When they open again, there is a deep sadness in them.

"You will not look at me the same way again, I promise you that."

Chapter Twelve

Barnaby

I WISH SHE WOULD not push me so much, but at the same time, it's something I enjoy about her. Maisie's mind is endlessly curious, always searching for answers. This must be why she is so good at her job.

I just have to hope that she'll reserve judgment—or if she does judge me, which she has every right to do, it will be merciful.

"After Eleanor drank from me, I died," I begin.

Maisie blinks. "Fully died?"

I nod. "My body was left in an alleyway. Police found me, and I was given an anonymous burial in a plain, wood coffin. It was buried underground with me inside it."

Her eyes grow huge and worried. I flap a hand at her.

"Don't concern yourself. Once Eleanor's blood worked its way through my system... it gave me life again."

"But you were buried!" Her mouth is agape.

"Yes. It took me some time to dig my way out. But my transformation had given me new strength, and I was able to do it."

"That must have been terrifying."

All I can do is nod in agreement. At the time, I thought I would never emerge. I thought I would die again, buried by six feet of earth.

"When I finally got free, Eleanor was waiting for me."

I remember vividly finding my murderer standing over my grave, a wicked smile on her ethereally beautiful face. She knew then that she was all I had, the only thing left in the world for me, and so I was already under her control.

I had been given a second life, and I owed it to Eleanor.

"She dragged me out of the dirt, and around us other vampires materialized, all to help me dig out my coffin."

Maisie leans forward on the ottoman. "So vampires really do sleep in coffins?"

I shrug. "It's tradition, I suppose."

She lets out an *ooh*, then falls quiet to let me continue.

"I was brought back to the coven and introduced to all seven members. Only a few others had been turned by Eleanor, too, and immediately they treated me as competition for her affection."

The worst part is that I understood it. The moment I looked upon Eleanor, I could feel her blood running through me, and it glued me to her side. I felt as if I would be nothing without her, and so I made myself her servant, begging and praying for an ounce of her attention.

I was so pathetic.

"What was the coven like?" Maisie asks.

I take a deep breath, steeling myself for what I have to tell her. But if I really want to court her, I ought to be honest with her about who I am.

"Bloodthirsty," I grind out. "They had just established themselves in Vienna and grown bold quickly. I was hungry—so hungry, back then—and so I... went along with everything they did."

My memory slides back to those dark nights in alleyways, finding a drunk on his way home in the dark and sinking my teeth into his throat.

Maisie's eyes are bright and innocent. "Like what? What did they do?"

Now is the moment. This is when she will get back into her futuristic car and leave the manse forever.

"I killed, Maisie." I fix my gaze on her as her eyebrows rise. "I was starving, and so I fed. I did everything and anything to get my hands on fresh blood, as new as I was to my second life. The craving took over my whole body and mind. I drank and drank, taking many souls."

She sits in place, staring at me with clear shock.

"Wow," Maisie says at last, bracing her hands on her knees as she leans forward. "Just like a baby, I guess. All you knew how to do was eat."

I blink. She has not gotten up to run. Not yet.

"I suppose so. An infant vampire. It took me some time to get past that stage of all-consuming thirst—many, many years. And under Eleanor's thumb, it was encouraged. We ravaged Vienna."

There is one thing I will not tell her, though. It is how we spent our days lying naked and covered in blood. I would be granted access to Eleanor, and then I'd slide my cock inside her while one of her other devotees slid inside me. That was often Jonathan, the vampire she turned after me. He would fuck me into Eleanor, faster and harder with every stroke, and I relished it. As none of us were capable of reproducing any longer, there was no need for hesitation or care. We reveled in our bodies, sinking our fangs into each other just as we did our victims and drinking until it was time to go on the hunt again.

"How did you escape?" Maisie asks, her voice quieter now. Still, she has not run.

This time is fuzzier for me. I was drunk on blood, fat and happy as a mosquito, when Eleanor found Penn.

"Penn," I begin. "He was just out of his child years, but to me, he still was a youth. It was Eleanor's decision to turn him that hardened me against her. She had stolen his entire life out from under him, and then brought him into our fold. He was innocent and young. He did not deserve it."

Just the memory of it stirs rage in me again.

"And I was a part of it. I lived in this horrid nest of ingrates, and I was responsible for Penn's fate as much as anyone's. I couldn't forgive Eleanor, and so I left. But I will always carry that guilt with me."

A soft touch on my shoulder brings me back to the present.

"You didn't make the choice to turn him," Maisie says, and I open my eyes to find her leaning toward me. She draws her finger down my arm to my hand and then takes it in both of hers. "Eleanor was the one in a position of power. Not you."

She's right, but I tire of this subject. I want to return to the fold of peace we had as Maisie ate dinner, to that bubble of lightness. I want to hold her in my lap and read sweet words into her ear.

"What then?" Maisie asks. "You managed to leave, and Eleanor didn't go after you?"

I wish it had been that simple. "I left the group when we went hunting one night. I had achieved greater control over my urges by then, so when I made the decision, I made it quickly. While the others were occupied with their meals, I returned to the house of an old friend, who had grown much older by then."

I think of the letter Maisie found in the desk drawer.

"He gave me Beatrice's letter. I made him promise never to tell her that he had seen me. He knew something was wrong, as he had aged while I hadn't."

She taps her chin. "And you've held onto it ever since."

"I left Vienna immediately and came to this country in hopes of hiding from her." Eleanor may still be out there now—she likely is. But I ran far enough away that I wasn't worth chasing.

"Now that I have answered your questions," I say, "may I show you the book?"

Maisie laughs and then, without prompting, picks herself up off the ottoman and settles in my lap. She feels marvelous there, her warm buttocks resting on my thighs. I hold the novel out in front of her and crack open the cover, releasing a puff of dust. Maisie sneezes, which has the lovely effect of pushing her body back against mine.

Almost immediately, my cock is alert, excited for this development. But I keep it at bay as Maisie settles into my shoulder and I begin reading the first page of the book.

Maisie

I could fall asleep listening to Barnaby's surprisingly soft voice as he reads to me. But I don't, because I'm interested in other things.

At the end of chapter one, as the hero and heroine have just met, I lean my head back and gently press my lips to his cheek. Barnaby's narration stutters for a moment, but then he continues.

I know what he's afraid of. He doesn't want to drink from me. His reluctance shouldn't hurt, but oddly, it does.

What if I *wanted* him to? Would he find me repulsive if I offered? Would he consider it a betrayal of all his values, everything he's worked for since leaving the coven, if I gave him the opportunity?

I take my kiss lower, down to the side of his throat, and this time he loses a whole word from the sentence he's reading. He goes back and rereads it, but I'm not listening anymore. There's a lump under his pants, right between my legs, and it's making me increasingly warm there.

"Barnaby," I murmur into his ear, and he pauses his reading. "Is this really what you want to be doing? Here, at your home, alone? Not that I mind it, but I think we could try some other things, too."

It's nearly imperceptible when his fangs lengthen, protruding from his lips.

"What sort of things?" he asks, voice low and husky.

To make my meaning clearer than words ever could, I roll my hips, grinding my ass against that bulge between his thighs. Barnaby gasps into my ear.

"I see." He drops his hands to my waist, bringing me down even more roughly against his lap. "Maisie. We must have a conversation."

"About what? I did, um, bring a condom. If you're, you know, worried about that."

A laugh escapes him, and I blush, shrinking into his arms.

"That is not an issue," Barnaby says, nuzzling my head with his nose. "My seed is, erm, no longer potent since my death. It is... my other desires that may get in the way. I don't want to hurt you."

"Why not?" I ask. "What if I was willing?"

Barnaby's hands on my waist fall perfectly still. "Please clarify."

I lean back, kissing his cheek again. "What if I wanted you to do it? What if..." I almost choke on the words because they're so embarrassing. "What if I wanted to feed you?"

There is no response, and I don't think Barnaby is even breathing. Then, his head lowers, and his breath whispers across my neck.

"What are you saying?" he asks hoarsely. "You *want* me to bite you? To hurt you?"

"I want you to feel good." To emphasize the point, I wiggle my ass, and his cock jumps under me. "If you're hungry and I can help, then I want to."

A shudder travels through Barnaby's body, and his arms wrap tight around me, like iron.

"You don't know what you're asking for." His lips pass over my throat, and my blood rushes faster through my veins.

"Yes, I do. I'm a grown woman." I lower my voice. "I trust you to stop before you drain me."

He breathes in sharply, and his cock grows thicker underneath me. Two cool incisors press to my neck, twin pinpricks of suggestion.

"Maisie," Barnaby rumbles. "I will be happy merely with a taste."

I rub my ass against his crotch, making him groan. "Then taste me."

"If that is truly what you want," he says in a low voice over my shoulder, "*truly*, then I would very much like to take you to bed with me."

Oh, fuck yes.

I nod vigorously. "Please."

He slips one arm under my knees, the other cradling my back, and swings me up into his arms as he rises to his feet. On instinct, I cling to his neck and squeak.

He lets out a huff of laughter. "I will not drop you," Barnaby says as he carries me out of the room, to the stairs.

"Wow. You're strong." I glance down at the floor beneath me. He's not a broad or a muscular man, but that clearly isn't stopping him.

His lip quirks. "One of the very few benefits of my second life."

He ascends the steps two at a time because his legs are so long, and veers down a hallway lined by a banister. He chooses a door, then uses his knee to push it open.

"Where are you taking me?" I ask. "You sleep up here?"

He chuckles. "Oh, no. My coffin is in the basement. But I'm not going to enjoy you in such a small space."

The way he says *enjoy*, like I'm a prime dessert, makes me shiver. I can't wait.

Chapter Thirteen

Barnaby

I GENTLY LAY MAISIE on the bed, all my blood boiling for what's to come.

She wants me to drink from her. That is the only thought in my mind—well, except what she'll feel like when I'm finally inside her.

But I have much I want to do before then. I haven't been on this earth for more than two hundred years to hurry such an encounter, especially when there is a good chance she may not want to repeat it. Once she experiences the truth of being with a vampire... I have my doubts Maisie will return to my home.

When she's prone in front of me, I reach down and unbutton my vest, watching as her chest heaves with each of her excited breaths. Her hazel eyes are alight, and her hands curl in the hem of her blouse. Once I've removed my vest, I take off my collared shirt and tie, setting them both over the back of a chair by the desk.

This is one of the many "guest" rooms in the manse, which have never been used. Until now.

Maisie's little pink mouth falls open as I turn back to face her, now shirtless, and she swallows thickly.

"Wow. You're really fucking hot."

The words take me by surprise. She sits up as she yanks her top up over her head and throws it off to the side, onto the floor. I'm tempted to pick it up and fold it, but I'm too distracted.

Under that baggy blouse is a slender body, with pert, pale breasts covered in freckles, bound up by a white brassiere. Her eyes connect with mine as she reaches behind her back and unhooks it, then drags it down her arm and tosses it on the floor along with her other clothing.

My breath sticks in my throat at the sight of her. I kneel at the side of the bed, a supplicant, and rest my hands on her hips. Then I trace up her sides to her ribcage, but hover before reaching any farther.

"Touch me," Maisie commands.

Like a puppet on strings, I do what she asks, sliding the pads of my fingers to the swell of her breasts. She inhales sharply as I cup them in my hands, then rove upward to cover her twin nipples. They're hard and pebbled in the cool air, and I wish I had turned up the heat before bringing Maisie here.

Perhaps next time I will make love to her beside the fire.

She moans prettily under me as I run my thumbs over those small peaks, trying to remember how this is done.

It's been so long since I seduced anyone that I'm not sure I can do it now. And yet my body is leading me anyway as I pinch her nipples between my thumb and forefinger and roll them about, dragging a rough gasp from Maisie's lips. While I play with her, her hands drop to the button of her baggy corduroys, which she unfastens and shimmies down her hips. When they reach her knees, I help to push them down and drag them off her feet. She kicks them away.

She is eager. She thinks I'm *hot*.

This time when I turn my attentions on her breasts, I do so with my mouth, rising onto the bed and pressing a knee onto the flower-patterned comforter. Seizing her nipple with my lips, I squeeze it until she's shuddering under me, then I move to the other side. I like how her breasts are ever so slightly different, one larger than the other. It's unique and charming.

"Barnaby," Maisie murmurs, petting my hair as I tongue her, then nibble with my teeth. Her back arches, so I hook one arm behind it, pulling her against me as I feast. "Ah! That's so good."

I like that she tells me what she enjoys, and it means I'm succeeding at pleasing her. An instinctual memory surfaces of other encounters I've had, reminding me what would please her even more.

With my other hand, I slip my fingers between her thighs, where her panties cling to her body. Immediately, she parts her legs, welcoming me in. I find a powerful heat waiting inside, and the fabric here is moist.

It sends a shiver straight from my neck to my cock.

She's already getting wet for me. And she's so wonderfully, blisteringly hot that my blood starts to thrum faster in my own veins. I can almost see how her own warm blood travels around her body, how more and more of it pools at the crux of her legs as I nurture her pleasure.

I have to have her there. But first, I brush my finger along the gusset of her underwear, pressing as I do to soak up even more of her juices.

"Mmm," Maisie hums as I continue lapping at her nipples and stroking her, moving my hand up and down over the tiny bump I feel underneath the fabric. Her hips jerk at each pass, and her hands cling to my shoulders.

When I finally pull away from her lovely breasts, Maisie seizes my mouth in a kiss. It's shockingly bold, but very welcome. I endeavor to be careful around her lips with my fangs, but it's a challenge with how prominent they've grown. Her tongue meets mine in the middle, and I can feel her desire rolling off her in the way our mouths fit together. I continue stroking between her thighs, faster and faster, and her kisses grow more urgent as she rocks her hips against my hand.

When I withdraw from our kiss, her lips are plumper and pinker than before. Some of her cute curls have fallen in front of her eyes, making her look tousled.

"Now yours," Maisie says, hooking her finger in the waistband of my slacks. I stand up straight as she takes my belt first, slinging it away carelessly, then unbuttons my pants and draws the zipper down. I help her slide them off, taking my underwear with them.

Her eyes go wide. "Oh, *wow.*"

I glance down at my cock, which gently curves toward her, wondering what's surprised her. I think about covering it from her gaping expression, but before I can move, her hands land on my bare flesh.

I reel from the sensation.

"What is it?" I ask with a gasp.

"You're, um, very big." Her tone is awestruck as her fingers circle my shaft. "Is that a benefit of being a vampire?"

I can only stare at her. "No, I was this way before."

Maisie shakes her head, disbelieving. "Incredible." As she strokes one hand up toward the head, I let out a gasp. "Maybe he was born that way, maybe it's Maybelline."

I don't know what this means, but it stops mattering as she lowers her head and, like a baby fawn by the side of a creek, darts out her tongue to lick me.

This was the very last thing I expected her to do, and it stuns me speechless as she drags her mouth around the head of my cock. I nearly buckle forward at the onslaught. Her hands both stay rooted to the shaft, squeezing and stroking as she explores. Maisie is so bold with her touch that I'm awed and blessed and utterly helpless.

Then she takes me deeper into her mouth, and a powerful surge of pleasure blows through me, straight into my bollocks. They seize, and I almost grab her hair in my hand in surprise. Instead, I pet it gently while she sinks even more of me in between her lips.

It's been so long since I had intercourse that I might just fire off. I need to buy myself some time.

"Maisie," I say gently, touching her shoulder. She looks up at me, and I almost explode just at the sight of pink lips spread around my cock, her small hands fisting the root. "Get up on the bed and lie back."

Her brow furrows, and she releases me with a *pop!*

"Do you not like it?" she asks.

I shake my head rapidly. "No, I like it very much. Too much. So, I need you to let go and lie back on the bed, like I told you."

Her eyes widen, and then a small smile pulls up the side of her mouth.

"Ooh, I like it when you do that," she says, though I'm not sure what *that* is. Obediently she lies down, spreading her legs for me. I love what a vibrant, sexual creature she is. It's not what I expected underneath all those heavy clothes of hers.

"What should I do now?" She plucks her nipples for me and wiggles her hips.

A smile pulls at my mouth. "Take off your undergarments," I instruct.

Maisie giggles. "*Undergarments.*" She slides the strip of fabric down and tosses it away, too. At last, she's completely bared to me, and I'm ready to eat her.

Her hair is darker below her waistline, curlier and denser and more of a reddish-brown. I kneel on the bed between her legs and study my bounty, licking my lips at the sight of how pink she is, how the lips of her small cunt have already swollen up. I like that she finds me attractive, so much that she's needy and wet.

Retaking her nipples, I attend to each of them before working my way southward, exploring her smooth belly to the thatch of hair beneath it. Maisie inhales sharply as I breathe her in. My fangs are as long as they can get, so ready to strike her, to drink from that thick artery running up the inside of her thigh.

Instead, I find her clit with my forefinger and gently brush over it. The response I get is a good one, so I touch it again, and again, then explore downward to ease my way. There she's soft and soaking, sweet fluid gathered all around her small slit.

I suck in a deep breath and then lick her. She lets out a moan and her hips jerk, so I do it again, just flitting the tip of my tongue over her clit. It's easy to work her up with these small teases, and I relish how sensitive and giving she is under my hands. If my cock is as she says, I'll need to warm her up. In the coven, we had sex rough and hard—almost like a torture we inflicted upon each other.

No, I want to be gentle with Maisie and her soft, yielding body until her blood is pumping fast.

I deepen my licking, twirling her sweet pearl around with my tongue until she's gasping and snapping her hips against my face. That's when I slide a finger inside her.

"Oh!" Maisie rewards me by getting even wetter around me. "Fuck, that's good!"

I love that she has no problem voicing her pleasure. It makes it satisfying to tuck that finger deeper inside her, exploring her, sampling the soft texture of her channel. Once I have a feel for her, I pump it slowly, taking my time to spread her open. Her body seizes under me, shaking and twitching as she gets closer.

But I want more. I fit another finger into her, and that small slit willingly gives, allowing me in. Maisie arches her back.

"Barnaby!"

My name sounds incredible in her sweet voice. I dive deeper into her as I devour her bud. My blood is flowing hotter now, my need almost overwhelming. My own hips grind against the bed as I sink into her, lavishing her with my tongue's attention, flicking back and forth as she writhes and cries out my name.

Maisie smells so, so wonderful. The most perfect flower, the most delicious meal—she is all of it. As her voice ratchets higher, and she tenses more and more around me, the need becomes nearly catastrophic.

Then her channel clamps down tight around me, and her voice comes out as a scream. I can't help it any longer. While I pump my fingers frantically inside her to urge on her finish, I turn my head, open my mouth, and sink my fangs into her thigh.

Chapter Fourteen

Maisie

I'M SCREAMING A FULL-THROATED scream as Barnaby bites me—*hard*. His fangs bury themselves in my flesh, and the sudden burst of pain catapults my orgasm into a tornado. I'm picked up and hurled around by it as he pulls his fangs free and presses his lips to the wound. With each of his sucks, with each thrust of his fingers inside me, I'm coming harder and harder. How is he doing that? Somehow, the bite of his fangs has unlocked a pleasure I never knew existed. I feel like my body might shrink into a single atom and then implode into nothing but dust.

When I come down, Barnaby slides his hand out of me. He gazes up over the mound of my pelvis as he licks his fingers dry. My mouth falls open at the sight of him with blood trailing down the sides of his lips. My blood.

Why is that so fucking hot?

Barnaby's dark eyes are glowing brightly as he climbs up the bed, placing his arms to either side of me. His pink tongue swipes the blood off his lips, and his lids close in bliss.

"You..." He swallows thickly. "You taste incredible, Maisie. Your cum and your blood on my lips are like nothing I've had in all my years." He even looks less pale now, with a fresh ruddiness to his cheeks.

I'm flying, absolutely soaring. No one's ever said something like that to me before. Well, not that I've ever had someone drink my blood, but still.

I reach up and stroke his cheek, and Barnaby leans into me as I lift my head to kiss him. Hungrily he kisses me back, his hips lowering to brush his cock over my belly. Now that I've returned to earth, I'm aching again, my pussy clenching as I breathe.

I need him. I need him right now, more than I've ever needed anyone. I need him to fill me, and then fuck me, and then maybe even bite me again as I orgasm because I've never flown so high in my life.

"Please," I whimper, snapping up my own hips to meet his. Barnaby groans and kisses me once more before sitting back on his knees to look down between my thighs. He palms his cock, stroking it as he gazes at me with hooded eyes.

"Spread your legs for me," he commands, and instantly I do. He guides himself down between them, and I feel his soft cockhead graze over my clit, then my folds, seeking the spot where he's most needed. As I wriggle under him, trying to bring him inside me, he rewards me by sinking just the tip of himself in.

Barnaby groans, stilling. He dips his head and kisses me, more tenderly this time, his chest heaving.

"You're so beautiful," he murmurs to me, pushing in slightly deeper.

I moan and arch up, trying to keep my eyes on his. He winds his hips back, fully leaving me, then slides farther in, his thick cock asking me to open for him.

And open I do. Whisked along by how wet I am, he glides through, and both of us moan at the same time as he buries himself shockingly deep.

"Fuck, Barnaby!" I grip his arms tight as the glorious stretch of him sends a wave of bliss straight to my brain. Experimentally he thrusts again, then again, sweat already beading on his forehead as he watches the place where we're connected.

"Your cunt is incredible," he manages between gasps. The word *cunt* makes me clench even tighter. "I can't..." His eyes smash closed and he buckles forward, landing on his elbow on top of me, so he's almost crushing me. He pauses his movement, breathing hard.

"I'm too close," he confesses, with an honesty that makes me smile.

"Let's just lie like this, then." I wrap my arms around his neck and bring him in so our mouths are almost touching. I lick one of his fangs, and Barnaby shudders from head to toe.

We lie like that, his cock sunk all the way inside me, just kissing. When he's gotten his breath back, my vampire opens his eyes and peers down into mine, the slightest smile on his lips.

"Now," he murmurs, lowering his lips to my ear, "I'm going to fuck you like I mean it."

Gathering me up close, Barnaby withdraws, then slams himself in with shocking force. When I cry out, he does it again, and again, drawing his hips back and then sinking in as deep as he can. Within moments, I'm completely lost to my bliss, gripping him tight as he takes me hard and fast, just like he promised.

But I need more. More, and more, and more. I want everything.

"Barnaby!" I cry out, weaving my hands through his hair and then holding on tight as I surrender to him. I bury my face in his neck because looking upon him, taking in the sharp planes of his face and the pride in his nose, is almost too much for me. He's handsome, and gentle, and so magnetic that I think...

I think there's a good chance I'm falling in love with him.

Barnaby

With how gloriously Maisie clenches around me, the only thing that keeps me from coming inside her right now is how hard I'm trying to keep the monster at bay. It's surging to the surface, clawing at the edges of the box I've placed it in, and it takes all my strength and willpower to keep from unleashing it.

But I will not let it out. I will not allow it to show its face in front of her.

I will not lose her.

Just as powerful is my need to drink her again. The taste of her blood is still on my lips, and it's the most perfect nectar this world has to offer. It fills my entire body with life, with fervor, and now I want nothing more than to make Maisie shiver and cry out underneath me.

I am utterly infatuated, completely ready to be her devotee. I remember when Eleanor demanded I fuck her, how emotionless and filthy it felt. This is a different plane of existence, where Maisie clings to me as if we're caught in a storm together and I'm her only life raft. She kisses me so tenderly and gazes at me with such affection in her eyes that I can't help but drown.

Where there was once gray shadow, there is now color. Everything is bright and vibrant around her, as if she generates a halo of pure life force.

I'm so close to the edge, toeing a steep cliff, that I grit my teeth and shut my eyes to keep my climax from erupting too soon. Even then I can smell her blood pumping wildly, hear her heart beating as fast as a rabbit's, and I desperately need more of her.

I can't control it. As Maisie throws her head back in pleasure, I lean down and pierce her flesh with my fangs for a second time.

Blood instantly wells to the surface, and Maisie's moan morphs into a scream of bliss. I pump more furiously as the sweet flavor of her fills my mouth. The monster is creeping closer, but as I feed, I'm able to push it back. I suck and suck, my thrusts speeding up as Maisie clenches tighter and tighter around me. Her wet heat sends a cataclysm of sensation into my bollocks, and I don't know how much longer I can resist.

And then her cries stop in her throat. Maisie's eyes grow huge and her mouth hangs open, and her entire body clamps down around me. There's nothing I can do now but let go.

One final time I slam into her, burying my cock as deep as I can, as my own orgasm races down my spine. I roar, an unexpected sound even for me, and grip her tight as it consumes me. I swell inside her and groan as my seed finally bursts forth, shooting everything deep in her body.

I collapse on top of her, keeping myself from crushing her with one hand. Maisie shivers all over as the remnants of her pleasure wind through her, and each pulse of her cunt around me causes my eyes to roll back in my head. I lick her blood off my lips, relishing the glorious, unparalleled taste of her.

"Damn," Maisie says at last, the fog clearing from her eyes. A wide smile takes over her face. "You're really, really good at that."

I can't help but smile back. "So are you." Feeling how tender and sensitive her swollen channel is, I work myself free gently, then collapse to the bed beside her. There's still blood dripping down her neck, though, and I belatedly remember that humans are much more delicate than my kind.

Quickly I get up, but Maisie reaches toward me. "Where are you going?" she asks, her smile falling.

"Wait one moment." I kiss her once on the lips before I pull away. Quickly I head downstairs, where my first aid kit is under a bathroom sink. It's never been used before. I return to the bedroom and Maisie sits up when I reappear, but I urge her to lie back down.

First, I attend to the wound on her thigh, spilling peroxide onto a cotton ball before wiping it over the twin punctures. Then I pull out a band-aid and stick it over the top.

Maisie giggles. "Oh. Thank you."

I shake my head. "No, thank you. No one... no one has ever given me a gift like this."

Though the smile on my face feels foreign, it's also *right*. There's a sense of joy, a pillar of life in me that I haven't felt since the very last time I drank human blood.

Maisie lets me see to her throat next, and the sight of my mark on her fills me with immense pride. She let me claim her. She let me drink from her.

She is perfect.

When I'm finished, I lie down at her side and bundle her up in my arms, bringing her close to my bare chest. She strokes me there, her head tucked neatly under my chin, until her hand slows and so does her breathing.

Soon, she's asleep, right next to me, right where she belongs.

A sudden realization washes over me.

This won't last.

She has already been here for more than a week, which means only a few more remain. After that... she'll leave me. After that, she'll go back home, wherever that is, and I won't see her again.

All my joy, all my pleasure at having her, is washed away. I will have to say goodbye to her when this is over, and every part of me objects to the idea.

I grit my teeth. I cannot become this attached. I cannot go through another heartbreak.

As good as her body felt around mine, I cannot let her inside, or it will destroy me when she finally goes.

Chapter Fifteen

Maisie

WHEN I WAKE UP the next morning, I'm tucked under a warm comforter, alone.

I sit up, looking around for any sign of Barnaby, but he's gone. In his wake, though, I can smell something absolutely marvelous in the air.

Bacon.

Leaping out of bed, I grab my clothes off the floor and hurriedly put them on. The smell has triggered a deep and powerful hunger in me, and I wonder if it's because of all the blood I lost last night. I desperately need food, and I need it now.

When I come down the stairs, I find Barnaby in the kitchen, flipping bacon over in a pan. In another pan, he's cooking what appears to be French toast. I'm giddy at the idea of so much food.

He glances up as I approach in my bare feet, and a slight smile tugs at the corner of his mouth. He's dressed, but not in his usual stuffy clothes. Instead, he wears a collared shirt with the top few buttons open, and soft pants cling to his rather perfect ass. I take him in, and for a moment, I wonder what it would be like to wake up to this every morning.

I approach him from behind and slip my arms around his waist. He tenses, though, so I release him.

"Are you all right?" I nuzzle his back with my nose. Barnaby sighs and lets one of his hands drop to mine, covering it where it rests across his belly.

"Yes."

Satisfied, I let him go and sit down at the table, where a cup of black coffee is waiting for me.

"Coffee?" I'm pleasantly surprised.

Barnaby glances at me over his shoulder. "I remember what it was like to have a fresh cup of hot tea in the morning. I figured you would want some."

"I didn't think you would *have* coffee," I say, sipping it. Oh, wow, that's good.

"I purchased some." He turns his head away with a somewhat bashful expression. "I didn't know if you would be staying over, but I wanted to be prepared if you did."

That warms me even more than the coffee does. He anticipated my needs, even though they are no longer his needs.

"Thank you." I say it as sincerely as possible. "This means a lot to me."

"No problem." He doesn't say anything else as he flips the French toast, so we fall into silence while he cooks. A few minutes later, he removes something from the oven, and brings over a plate with bacon, eggs, and toast, then sets it in front of me. He sits at the table, too, and there's a color in his face I've never seen before.

"You look good," I remark as I stuff some bacon in my mouth. "And this is heavenly."

"Good." Barnaby nods. "I'm glad it pleases you."

It's utterly perfect, but he doesn't speak while I eat. When I'm finally finished, I offer to clean up, but he refuses again.

"Adeline will take care of it later," he says. "I need to go open the store soon."

Understanding that it's time to leave, I quickly wash my face and slip on my shoes.

"Would you like a ride into town?" I ask him.

Barnaby shakes his head. "The walk will do me good."

It's a very long way, but I don't argue. Still, it makes me a little sad. I had wanted to prolong this, to spend more time with him, but I get the sense that he needs his space.

"All right."

When it's time to leave, he gives me a light kiss at the front door, and it closes behind me.

The rest of the day, I'm in a daze. All I can think about is Barnaby, how it felt to lie underneath him, to take him inside me with his fangs sunk into my flesh. How did that feel so good? It made my orgasm ten times more intense.

I want him to drink from me every time.

Hiking feels like it'll take far too much energy, so I decide instead to explore the cove. There's a small boat that conducts tours, and I sign up for one before boarding with a life jacket on.

It's an easy trip, and I can zone out listening to the tour guide as she points out each landmark around the cove. We're given fishing rods, and a few of the other tourists manage to land a fish.

"Be careful," she tells us. "There are mermaids here. Sometimes they get grumpy with us if we fish too far out."

I kind of hope I see one. I wonder what a mermaid looks like up close.

As I head back to my apartment that afternoon, I stop at the bookstore to see Barnaby. He's alone, as usual, reading a book behind the counter.

"Hi," I say when I step inside.

Barnaby glances up. "Oh, hello." He sounds unusually cheery. "Have a nice day?"

"Oh yes! Saw the cove, and it was lovely. There's so much to do and see, and it's so beautiful."

When he smiles, it's surprisingly big and carefree. "That natural beauty is the reason I decided to stay here when I found it. Very few places on earth can offer both the sea and the mountains."

He's absolutely right. Somehow I stumbled across the perfect vacation.

Remembering that, though, brings down my mood. I've already spent a week and a half here. That leaves just a few weeks until I have to leave again—which means abandoning whatever is budding between us.

It makes my stomach sour to think about. But it also means I can't waste any time.

"What are you doing after you close up shop?" I ask, sidling up to the counter. I take a quick peek out the front window to see if anyone's watching, and then lean toward Barnaby, resting on my elbows.

He quirks an eyebrow before he leans against the counter, too, bringing our faces rather close together. "I have not made plans. Well, outside of reading."

"You could read me another chapter of that book." I lower my lashes and bat them. His left brow rises. "They'd only just met when we stopped. I want to see the fireworks."

He seems to realize a little late what I'm insinuating, and his mouth turns up at one side. "I see. I suppose we could read together again."

"I'd like that."

Checking once more that we aren't being watched, I lean forward and peck him quickly on the lips. Barnaby jolts, but I'm already backing away and giving him a tiny wave.

"I'll see you later?" I ask in a singsong voice.

He rubs his lips like he's mystified by what I just did, then he slowly nods. "Yes. I'll close at ten, and we can drive there together."

"Great."

I'm ecstatic. He wants a repeat. Most of the time when I hit it off with a guy, I never see him again, so this is a wonderful change of pace.

After quick goodbyes, I head back out of the bookstore, humming a tune under my breath. I might only have a few weeks left, but I'm going to make the absolute best of them.

Someone gasps as I bump into them. I wasn't paying attention at all to where I was going, and now I'm face-to-face with a small, plump woman wearing a bright pink dress and a straw sun hat.

"Oh, gosh, I'm so sorry," I say, backing away. "I wasn't looking where I was going, and—"

"Quite all right!" The woman peels down her sunglasses to get a look at me. "Didn't find anything you wanted at the bookstore?" She glances down at my empty hands.

I stare at her. "Huh?" Then I realize she probably thinks I'm a customer. "No, no. I've already bought, like, three books there. But I'm kind of friends with the owner, and I live upstairs, so—"

The woman gasps. "You're the renter!" She claps her hands together, and her face is alight. "And you're *friends* with Barnaby? Isn't that lovely!"

I feel immediately like I've done something wrong. He will not like this, whatever it is.

"Uh, yeah, I guess so." I tilt my head, trying to figure out who this woman is. "What's your name?"

"My apologies." She tucks her sunglasses away into her purse, then extends a hand to me. I shake it, and her grip is surprisingly firm. "I'm Louise, mayor of Hallow's Cove."

I balk. The fucking *mayor*? Great. And she probably just saw Barnaby and me making out.

"No need for that look." She winks at me. "I'm glad to see our resident grouch branching out. It's good for him."

"He's wonderful," I say. I don't like that she called him a *grouch*. "Very, um, accommodating. And welcoming." Right. He is my landlord, technically.

This only seems to please the mayor even more. Her eyes flick to the bandage on my neck, and she looks like she might just burst with excitement.

"I love to hear that. Maybe you could convince him one of these days to open the antique shop? The street fair was such a success, we're thinking about hosting one every other week on Thursdays."

I grimace at the thought. I don't get the sense Barnaby wants strangers poking through his furniture.

"Just drop the hint," Louise says, barreling onward. "That place has been shut up for too long. It needs some air."

She's not wrong about that. Some of those antiques probably need to be cleaned to help preserve them.

"All right," I say noncommittally. "I'll try."

A wide smile pinches her round cheeks. "Thank you. I think it would be a fun thing for tourists, you know? There's so much history there."

"Sure." I doubt Barnaby will go for the idea, though.

Suddenly, the woman's face *changes*. On top of her neck is now Barnaby's head—a perfect replica. She imitates his voice as she says, "I don't want greasy hands all over my antiques!"

I gape at her, completely taken aback. Then Louise shifts to her original face, with its plump cheeks and plump lips.

"I know, I know," she continues, rolling her eyes. "But I'm sure you can convince him." She turns on her heel. "Well, I hope you enjoy the rest of your stay in Hallow's Cove. Don't hesitate to call the mayor's office if you need anything!"

With that, she continues off down the sidewalk without even waiting for a response. I stare after her, feeling like I was just hit by a hurricane.

Huh. A mimic, I guess.

Finally, I'm free, so I decide to get a big dinner and stock up for tonight. If Barnaby wants to feed on me again, I'll need to be prepared.

Lots of iron, you know.

Chapter Sixteen

Barnaby

I DID NOT ENJOY watching Louise talking with Maisie in front of the shop. The mayor was so animated, who knows what secrets of mine she spilled while chatting Maisie's ear off? When she's gone, I grumble and go back to my reading. At least Louise didn't feel the need to come in and bother me.

No, the last thing I want is for the mayor to ruin my good mood. Since drinking real, sweet, human blood again, I feel light and airy. My body is strong, and it's as if a fog has been lifted from everything. The world is sharper, clearer, and brighter. I see possibility and potential everywhere. First thing this morning I swept the whole shop, then dusted the tops of the shelves, not having realized how dirty they were.

And then when Maisie came in to visit after her trip around the cove? I wanted to drag her over the counter and kiss her, and then probably make love to her again.

Even though the mark on her neck is now covered with a bandage, seeing it there made my cock shiver.

That was *me*. I claimed her, I drank from her, and now she's—

I stop myself before I can even finish the thought. Now she's what? Mine?

The possessiveness of this phrase makes me growl. Maisie isn't mine. She can't be. She's human, and she's temporary.

Unbidden, I remember how Eleanor spoke of humans. *Prey.* In her eyes, we were superior to them, and they served no greater purpose than to feed us.

I shut my eyes. I'm not that version of myself any longer.

But it's still true that she is temporary here—that she plans to leave after the results of the investigation. I know it's not wise to get attached, but I couldn't stop myself from agreeing to meet with her again.

The rest of the day, I'm lost in a daydream about what tonight will be like. I think of reading quietly into Maisie's ear, about taking her clothes off again, about sipping from her like a glass of sweet wine while our bodies speak to each other.

I serve a few customers, but no one comes in after eight. Eventually I close up shop, turn off the lights, and step out onto the sidewalk. Then I knock at Maisie's door.

When she appears, she's like magic incarnate. She's wearing a *dress*, which seems very unlike her. It's robin's egg blue, has a swooping neckline, and a frilly skirt that ends just above her knees.

I unabashedly stare at her.

"Do you like it?" she asks, playing with the skirt. "One of those things you buy and then never wear. But I thought, reading a romance novel in front of the fire? Seems like as good a time as any."

I'm enchanted. Gone is the baggy camisole with the bulky pants. This number hugs her body closely, showing off every last curve of it, and instantly I want to tear it off her.

It will be more of a challenge tonight to keep the monster locked up. Already it's thirsting, drooling as I gaze upon her. Her face is expectant, waiting.

"I love it," I finally say. I trail a finger from her bare shoulder down to her hand, and she trembles in the night air. Cradling her fingers in mine, I drink in the sight of her a second time. "I can't say that I have a meal planned this time, though." I didn't think Maisie would invite me to spend time with her again so soon.

She flaps her other hand at me. "No worries. I'll get something to go from the diner."

We walk there side by side, and Lerana unabashedly stares at me as Maisie and I enter with our hands twined together. She hurries over to take our order, and I wish I could tell her to at least attempt to hide her shock and awe.

Maisie snorts next to me. "She looked like her eyes were about to pop out of her head."

It's truly adorable, that snort.

We wait for Maisie's food, then take it in a bag back to my house with us. We drive in her car once again, but this time she navigates the potholes a little better. When we reach my manse, she hops out like a rabbit and retakes my hand, as if she can't bear to be apart.

She doesn't eat her dinner until a few hours later, after we are both soaked in sweat and Maisie is shivering from the fierce power of her orgasm. This time, I sank my teeth into her breast as I was sucking on it, and she clamped down around me so powerfully that I came on the spot, still drinking from her while I spilled inside her.

I don't think there's anything in the world like consuming fresh blood while a beautiful woman screams underneath you. Then I pumped her so full that it dripped out all over the comforter, and I realized I would need to wash it myself if I didn't want Adeline to bear witness to my erotic activities.

After Maisie eats and we've cooled the heat in our veins, we sit in front of the fire on my Queen Anne and I read her the next two chapters of our book, until she's fallen asleep in my arms.

Should I tell her the truth about me? Or can I simply hide it until our time together is over, and she never has to know what monster lurks deep down inside?

The harder I fall for Maisie, the more wrong it seems to keep it from her. My true form longs to rise to the surface whenever we're together, and it's growing more and more difficult to hold it back.

Would she run in fear? Or is she, perhaps, stronger and sturdier than I give her credit for, and I should let her make the choice for herself?

Maisie

A week goes by in a flash. I'm trying to hold onto time, to keep it from slipping through my fingers, but it's like trying to catch a jellyfish. It oozes through, going onward without stopping and only moving faster the happier and more at home I feel here in Hallow's Cove.

Still, I await the results of the investigation, wondering if I'll still have a job when this is all over.

A clear change has come over Barnaby since he began drinking my blood. His skin is warmer to the touch. He smiles far more and has even become less snappy with his customers.

Yep. I'm definitely falling for that fucking vampire. And I think his good mood says he might be falling for me, too.

But I won't hope. That's not what either of us needs. We haven't talked about it yet, but we both know I'm leaving in a couple of weeks, and that's when all of this will come to an end. Though sometimes at night, when I'm curled up at Barnaby's side, my head resting on his smooth, naked chest, I wonder if it has to.

During the day I go on hikes, and now that I'm done with my second fantasy novel, it's time to tackle the Anne Hadron. I sigh while lugging it up the mountain, hoping it's not as tedious as the "romance" novel Barnaby reads to me in the evenings. We're nearly ten chapters in and they still haven't shared a kiss, and all the old-timey writing is boring. But I do it for him because he clearly enjoys reading to me, and I'm happy when he's happy.

I'm surprised when the Anne Hadron novel isn't at all what I thought. It has dark themes but a bright setting, and instantly I'm immersed in the world of the late nineteenth century, when the book takes place. Hadron is a good writer, and I think I know why Barnaby likes it. She takes care with the details while weaving a fascinating story about an elderly woman whose husband has just passed away, and she's traveling Europe looking for the answers to her life.

After a few hours, I realize I've sat there so long that now my skin is burned, so I reapply my sunscreen and head back down the mountainside.

When I reach the bookstore, I find Barnaby and Mayor Louise standing outside, discussing something rather intimately.

"Ah, the tenant!" Louise pivots when she sees me. "I was just speaking to Barnaby about the next street fair, and how lovely it would be if he opened up his antique shop as a display room. Don't you agree?"

I shoot a look at Barnaby, not sure what he wants me to say. He appears resigned.

"It could all use a good cleaning," I hedge. "What if we cleaned it together, Barnaby? The street fair would be a side bonus."

He searches me with his eyes, then rolls them and turns back to the mayor.

"Fine. Since Maisie is helping me, I'll do it. But it will be *no children allowed*. I cannot have them getting their sticky hands all over my priceless valuables."

"Of course, of course," Louise says, but I don't think she has any plans to enforce that. "It will be so lovely to see all your treasures out in the open."

She winks at me and then trundles off, calling out to someone else down the street.

"Thank you for nothing," Barnaby says to me when she's gone, but he's smiling. "I guess that means we'll spend the next two days dusting furniture."

"Then you can tell me about each piece!" I follow him into the bookstore. "I'm sure there's so much history there."

He shakes his head, chuckling. "Endlessly curious." A hand with long, thin fingers curls around my waist, pulling me to Barnaby's side. He kisses the top of my head. "Always wanting to know the truth of things."

"It's the bug-hunter in me. I want to know all the whys and hows. It helps me understand the world. And I really don't like surprises."

Barnaby's hand tightens around mine as we pause in front of the door at the back of the store, which leads into the room where he keeps his antiques.

"Maisie..." He hovers there, not looking at me. "Will you come over tonight so we can talk?"

I blink at him. "Well, I was planning on it, just like every other night so far."

He nods sharply. "Good." Then he releases my hand and opens the door, leading me into the darkness. He flips on a light switch, illuminating the sprawling collection of furniture. It's going to take a lot of legwork and elbow grease to clean this up, but I'm excited about the prospect of spending that much time with my vampire.

Mine. I know he's not, but I'm going to keep living in my fantasy world as long as I can.

Barnaby

The longer I wait, the worse it will be when I finally show her the creature—so I should do it sooner rather than later and let her judge me.

Maisie and I work for a good portion of the afternoon and into the evening, clearing dust off desks and dressers, vacuuming cushions and upholstery, and sweeping the floors. Maisie works hard, and even the scent of her sweat is utterly intoxicating. All I want to do is bend her over a couch and slide inside her. Her warmth has become home to me, and I long for it all day long as we labor over this room full of memories.

That, at least, dulls the ache in my chest as we uncover more and more of my past. Each item in my collection is linked to some event or person, many I want to forget. But somehow, with Maisie's light in the room, the shadows connected to them are much less dark. She asks me about each piece as we clean, and I offer what I can. I obtained a mirror from the early twentieth century that came from a duchess whose husband left her, and she had to sell off everything she owned to pay her bills.

Maisie gasps when she sees the image of us both standing in front of it. "I thought vampires didn't have reflections!" she says, awed.

I stare at her. "What?"

"Well, you know the myth, right? That someone's a vampire if they don't have a reflection?"

"That is physically not possible." I squint at her. "You believed this? You are good at math and science, or so I thought."

Maisie huffs. "Well, yeah. I didn't know any better. But I guess you're right—you're flesh and blood, so of course you have a reflection." She cocks her head at me. "Are you afraid of crosses?"

She really believes all these silly rumors?

"Why would I be afraid of a cross?" I ask. "It is merely a physical object."

She sighs. "Okay, never mind."

I've always found these superstitions about us terribly fascinating, especially the cross. I wasn't a religious man when I was alive, but I have thought about how I might be greeted in the afterlife after all I've done, all the heinous crimes I've committed against humanity, and I don't like to think about it.

"Wait, wait." Maisie stands up straight. "What about *garlic*?"

Wrinkling my nose, I lift the desk and place it off to one side, then open the drawers to check them for any other lingering remnants of my former life. "I don't care for it, but human food doesn't do much for me anymore."

She just shakes her head, giggling. "Of course. It seems like nothing I know about vampires is true."

Little does she know.

Chapter Seventeen

Maisie

When the sun has long set and it's nearly midnight, we decide to call it. I tell Barnaby that I could really use a shower after all our work, and he offers to let me use his, even though my apartment is right upstairs. I already know what he has planned, and I relish the idea of him fucking me senseless in the shower.

He doesn't bite me every time we have sex because he knows my body needs time to heal and recover. Luckily, though, the wounds heal exceptionally fast, leaving only the faintest of pink marks behind.

Something I'll always be able to remember him by.

When we leave the shop, I'm surprised to find the town is brightly lit. I glance up to find a huge full moon sitting high in the sky, casting everything in silvery light.

"Wow!" I grab Barnaby's arm and point. "That's amazing."

He smiles down at me, stroking my hand. "It's lovely when there are no other lights to compete with it."

I think he's right. The moon and stars would never look like this in the city. There's something magical about Hallow's Cove, and again the thought flits through my mind: what would it be like if I stayed here?

I already work from home. Internet is really all I need to do my job—if I even get to keep that job.

If I get fired, that gives me even less reason to return to my stuffy condo. I'd have to find another job, but I could easily see myself pouring coffee at the coffee shop, or perhaps helping Barnaby stock books. What if I spent more time on my game and sold it to a larger company? That could support me for a while.

But I don't mention these thoughts because I don't want to scare him off, either. I've known too many men who are afraid of commitment, and I worry that bringing up anything more permanent could ruin what we already have.

As we drive down the dark road toward Barnaby's mansion, a sudden streak of shadow blazes across the path. I slam on the brakes, afraid of hitting a deer and destroying my car. Both Barnaby and I fly forward in our seats, but the seatbelt jerks me back again, sending a ricochet of pain through my spine.

"Fuck!" I moan as I straighten my neck, then glance around for any sign of the deer. "What the hell was that?"

Barnaby's eyes narrow.

"Maisie," he growls. "Stay here." He climbs out of the car, his whole body tense in a way I've never seen it before.

I gape after him. "Stay here? Why? What was that, Barnaby?" Of course, I ignore him, opening my own car door to peer around the dark woods.

"Maisie!" Barnaby glares at me over the hood. His eyes are bright and glowing in the night, like those of an animal. "Get back in the car!"

He's never bossed me around like this, not outside the bedroom, and I don't like it. I grab my keys, where I keep the bear spray I bought, and aim the canister.

"Don't worry about me."

He groans with annoyance, but then a crunching sound off in the trees grabs his attention. Barnaby moves around the car toward me, eyes transfixed on a point off to our left, keeping his body in front of mine.

"Come out!" he calls into the darkness. "I know you're there!"

Why is he attracting attention to us? Maybe I really should have stayed in the car.

"It was just a deer." I place a comforting hand on Barnaby's arm. But he shakes me off, and when he glowers at me again, his face looks... different. His brows are more severe, his fangs long and sharp.

"It is no deer," he snarls in a voice that's much deeper than usual.

That's when I hear it: twigs snapping, followed by a low growl. Oh, fuck. Whatever it is, it definitely isn't a deer.

"Bear!" I call out in warning. "Get back in the car, Barnaby!"

He shakes his head. "A car will not protect us from this, if it is what I think it is."

From out of the shadows, something finally appears. It's tall, far too tall to be any sort of human. Fur covers its body, the shaggy ends highlighted by the moon's glow. Pointy ears flatten against its head, and yellow eyes glow in the dark.

"Vampire," the creature says, voice low and husky. When it takes another step out into the light, I know what it is.

A werewolf.

The werewolf is enormous, with dagger-like claws and white fangs so long and so sharp it could tear me to ribbons without much effort. I gasp and shrink behind Barnaby, wishing that I'd listened to him and stayed in the car.

Not that a car door could stop something this size. He was right about that.

"Do not come any closer," Barnaby warns the monster, and there's an ethereal hollowness to his voice. His fangs protrude from his mouth, sharp and white. "I will not hesitate to kill you."

A laugh tumbles out of the werewolf's mouth. "What are you going to do, vamp?" it asks, ignoring Barnaby's command as it takes another step toward us. "Bite me with your little teeth?"

Fear floods my nervous system, and all I can think about is how far I would have to run to lose a creature like this. But the rational side of me knows there's no way I could possibly outmaneuver it, not when it has legs that long and powerful.

"Do not make me take drastic measures." Barnaby's shoulders are coiling tighter, as if he's preparing to strike. What could he possibly do to fight such an immense beast?

"Hmm," the werewolf says. "Your human looks mighty delicious."

When it takes yet another step in our direction, Barnaby squares his body. And then... he starts to grow.

"I don't know what you are doing in my town," Barnaby snarls as his legs lengthen and his shoulders spread apart, "but I will make sure it is the last decision you make."

I step back, butting up against the car door as Barnaby continues to sprout into the air high above me. He roars as two objects emerge from his back, ripping through his shirt and vest. His clothes are splitting open, and even his feet have torn his shoes to shreds as they become... claws?

"Barnaby?" I whisper as terror fills me.

The protrusions on his back elongate and then spread open, revealing two immense wings. His flesh has even changed color from his usual pale, human skin tone to white, now laced with pinkish veins. Two sharp points grow out of his head, lengthening into fearsome horns, and his ears widen and spread open, like those of a bat.

Barnaby isn't a vampire. He's a *monster*.

I grab the handle of the car door and yank it open, then jump inside. Barnaby—or the creature that used to be Barnaby—flicks a look at me over his shoulder, and the sight of his face tears a shriek from my throat.

He has utterly changed. Now he has two rows of sharp teeth in his mouth, and his eyes are a fierce, glowing red. His brows are heavier, and his legs have reversed in angle, like that of an animal. His white hands now bear huge claws, even bigger than the werewolf's.

"Fuck," I hear the werewolf say just as I slam the door. Then there's a flash of white. A flap of Barnaby's massive wings rockets him forward, toward the werewolf, and he leaps onto his prey, shoving him down to the ground. Then the monster-formerly-known-as-Barnaby swipes with one huge hand, tearing open the flesh of the werewolf's chest.

The furry creature howls in pain, writhing on the ground. But he doesn't lie prone for long. Soon he fights back, pushing Barnaby's huge form off him before rolling away. Now freed, he leaps back to his feet, crouching on all fours.

Barnaby rises to two legs once more, the light of the moon highlighting every feature of him. Pink and red lines trail all across his white skin, as if he's been deprived of sunlight for eternity. His wings are massive, each one casting a long shadow on the ground.

For a moment, my fear recedes. He is strange but also... magnificent. I'm awed as much as I am horrified.

Barnaby strikes again, moving as fast as lightning. He rushes the werewolf, but it skids out of the way. Each of the two beasts attack and then feint, lashing out at one another with claws and fangs. I feel like I should do something, anything, to help Barnaby—but what could that possibly be?

The car. I press the button to start it just as the werewolf strikes. Barnaby's roar of agony sends goosebumps erupting across my skin. He is clearly powerful in this form, but is he stronger than a werewolf on the full moon?

When I back up the car, Barnaby's gaze darts to mine, confusion written across his face. While he's distracted, the werewolf lunges again, wrapping his huge, fanged maw around Barnaby's arm.

That's it. I won't stand by and watch this happen. I turn the wheel, aiming the front of my car right at the furry monster, and slam my foot on the gas. The car lurches, and as these electric vehicles do, instantly barrels forward at full speed.

Within half a second, there's a terrible *crunch!* as the front of my car smashes into the werewolf's bulky body. He lets out a horrid whine, but he's so big that even the car's spinning wheels can't seem to knock him over.

However, it does buy us a few moments without the werewolf on the attack. I put the car into reverse again, intending to ram the beast a second time, but Barnaby moves even faster. He wrenches the werewolf up to its feet by its throat, gripping it with both hands, blood still dripping down his arm.

"You will not hurt my woman," Barnaby snarls, squeezing his enemy's neck. "And you will not corrupt my town."

With incredible force, Barnaby hurls the werewolf into a nearby tree. The body slams against the trunk and he crumples, sliding down to the ground. Barnaby stalks toward the motionless object, fangs bared, and crouches down with claws out. I think he plans to rip open the werewolf's body.

Then I remember the man at the bar. The yeti had hinted he just recently turned, which explained his unhinged behavior.

This must be him, and he doesn't know how to control himself—the same way that once upon a time, freshly reborn as a vampire, Barnaby only knew how to feed.

"No!" I leap out of the car. "Barnaby, don't!"

He pauses with his mouth mere inches from his victim's throat.

"Don't kill him," I say, grabbing onto Barnaby's huge, veined arm. His skin is cold to the touch, and eerily smooth. "He's not a bad guy. He's just new. He can't control himself."

The massive, white monster stares at me with those huge, glowing eyes, and for a split second, I wonder if he might turn on me. I drop his arm and back away, my throat bobbing.

Then, his eyebrows tilt down, and he rises back to his feet.

"Maisie." His voice comes out a growl. "The wolf could wake up at any time."

"He's... he's not going to attack us," I say, my voice quiet and frightened. "I think we're safe now."

Barnaby's wings lower, and then slowly fold up against his back. He glances at the werewolf one more time, baring his teeth as if daring him to get up again.

He doesn't.

I shrink back against the car as Barnaby turns his full attention toward me. He must be eight feet tall like this, and he's completely, utterly naked. His muscles are swollen and defined, though they're strange in their anatomy. The only thing on his body that isn't white are his horns, which are black and curl up and over his head.

All I can do is stare, though I carefully avoid looking between his legs.

"Maisie." Barnaby's voice is so strange and foreign, but I can still tell it's him under there. He takes a step in my direction, and I press myself harder against the car. "I'm... I'm so sorry you had to see me like this. I didn't mean for it to happen." He looks away, his body tense. "I had to protect you."

A warmth fills my chest. So that's what triggered this, whatever it is.

"What are you?" I finally ask, my heart beating a rapid tattoo in my chest.

His eyes fall to the ground, and his shoulders sag. He kneels so he can look into my eyes but doesn't move closer. "This is my true form, Maisie."

My hand is shaking as I raise it. I hope he doesn't kill me. I have to believe it really is Barnaby, that he would never hurt me. My fingers land on his cheek and he flinches, but he doesn't move away. Then he lifts his own massive, clawed hand to cover mine. I shudder underneath him, but he makes no further movement.

"Your *true* form?" I stare at him with my mouth open. "You've been hiding it all this time?"

"I didn't want to frighten you. But I had no choice tonight. I should have told you sooner."

My heart softens toward him. Of course he would hide this given how terrifying it looks at first glance.

I can't help a manic giggle. "So you appear in mirrors, and you're not afraid of crosses or garlic, but you turn into, um, this?"

A slight smile pulls at his lips, revealing his monstrous fangs. "Yes. This is the real secret vampires are hiding. You're probably the first to see this form and live to tell about it."

A shudder travels through me.

"Wow." I kneel, too, and scoot closer to him. It's clear Barnaby is ashamed of what he looks like, and I don't want him to feel that way about himself.

"This form is strange, but also beautiful," I say, stroking his cheek.

He blinks those red eyes at me. "Beautiful?"

"Terrifying. Majestic. Special."

Barnaby leans into my hand, and then suddenly his arms are around me, pulling me tight to his chest. He heaves with the force of his labored breaths.

"Maisie." His voice is thick with emotion. "Thank you."

I wrap my arms as far around him as I can and hold him like that, this huge monster. My monster.

Chapter Eighteen

Barnaby

SHE'S LETTING ME HOLD her. Maisie has gone limp in my arms as I clutch her close, fear and adrenaline still coursing through my veins from the werewolf's attack.

I thought I might lose her. I thought he would get past me and then wrap those fangs around her throat the way he did my arm. The rage is still there, bubbling just under the surface, and until it goes away… the monster, my true form, will remain.

My senses are much keener now, though, and eventually the scent of Maisie's fear ebbs. Her heartbeat slows, and she relaxes against me.

"Barnaby." Her hands curl tighter around my back. "You saved me."

"Of course I did." My tongue sticks in my mouth before I can say the other part, that I would do anything to save her, because I love her.

"Thank you," she says quietly.

Eventually, I release her and help her back to her feet. Maisie stares up at me, awe still painting her face.

"Wow. You're super tall." Her eyes travel down my broad chest, over the defined muscles of my abdomen, to...

When she reaches my groin, her eyes grow huge. "Whoa."

I follow her gaze downward and find that unfortunately, thanks to her rather close proximity just now, my cock is starting to swell and thicken. It's still hanging down, but not for long.

"Sorry." I glance around for the remnants of my clothes, but they're in shreds all over the forest floor. Instead, I try to cover it with my hand, but it's too big.

"I-it's okay." Maisie swallows hard, her eyes not leaving my crotch. Finally, she seems to realize what she's doing and jerks her head up. "Sheesh, I'm sorry. I'm ogling you."

I cock my head. "Ogling?"

She flushes, and her heart rate speeds up again. I can hear it pattering fast in her chest. "You know. Admiring your junk."

"*Admiring?*" Now I'm all types of perplexed. "It's ugly. And... disgusting."

At this, Maisie's brows furrow. "What? It's not ugly." She grabs my wrist and pulls my hand away defiantly. I allow her to do it. "I think it's cute."

I gape, unable to even ask for clarification. She thinks my true form's cock is *cute?*

"I mean," she adds, stumbling over herself. "It's too big to be cute. It's, um, cool? It's neat. I mean, I like it."

She reaches up to cover her face with her hands, hiding herself from me.

She likes it.

She actually *likes* it.

"You're saying this to placate me," I say, backing away. "You don't need to, though. I know this form is horrifying."

Maisie frowns at me, and it's a rather judgmental frown.

"No, it's not." She surveys me, from my horns all the way down to my clawed toes. "You're pretty cool like this. Plus, you absolutely kicked that werewolf's ass. It was hot."

That word again. A rush of pleasure shoots through me. She really doesn't mind seeing me like this? Despite the rumors about vampires, I've seen myself in the mirror. I know that I look like death and the devil and a bat all stewed together.

But she saw my cock. She said it was nice. Her cheeks heated, as if she was shy to admit it.

Now I'm well and truly hard.

"Barnaby…" Maisie's eyes have traveled downward again. "Is this turning you on?" Instead of backing away, as I expect, she takes a step toward me.

I freeze in place because I can't hide it. "Yes. I'm always turned on by you. Especially when you look down there."

Her eyes snap up to mine. "Sorry."

"Don't be sorry." I reach out and push one of her wild curls back from her face. "You can look at me as long as you like."

"Could I touch you?"

That's the very last thing I expected her to ask. I raise an eyebrow.

"You want to touch *that*?" My cock lifts its head even higher and now it's beginning to extend toward her, searching for that promised touch.

Maisie nods, her eyes twinkling in the moonlight. When I give her a brief, disbelieving nod, she takes a step closer. She peers down at my cock, which is the same white as the rest of my skin. Her small hand reaches out and wraps around it, and the sensation of her warm flesh against my cold skin almost undoes me instantly.

"Maisie," I groan as she tightens her grip. I buckle forward, overwhelmed by it.

"Does it hurt?" she asks, worried.

"No, no." I let out a sharp breath. "The opposite."

She grins, and her first hand is joined by her second one. I know the werewolf passed out nearby could wake up at any time, but I don't want to stop her, not when she begins to stroke the length of me, from the thick root to the swollen tip.

Then Maisie kneels in the pine needles, and to my absolute shock and incredible awe, she opens her mouth and circles me with her lips.

I'm stunned and disbelieving as she takes as much of me in as she can on her first try. She giggles against my cock as she sucks on it, stroking her hands in time with her lips. I nearly topple forward, and I brace my hands on my thighs just so I don't crush her.

"Maisie," I moan, unconsciously tangling my claws in her hair. I try to move away after realizing I've touched her with my huge, clawed hand, but she leans into me instead. Her mouth pumps faster, and I'm so close to the edge already that I don't know if I can hold on without sliding off the cliff.

"Wait." I touch her cheek, and Maisie pauses, looking up at me. I'll never get tired of how beautiful she looks with her lips spread wide open, her cheeks hollowed out. "I'm going to finish if you keep going. Right here, in the woods." I glance around us.

She blinks those beautiful hazel eyes and gently removes my cock from her mouth. After licking her lips she says, "Would you rather finish inside me?"

The bottom drops out of my stomach. She can't be saying what I think she's saying.

"Inside... you?" I echo, not sure I heard her right.

Maisie peers down at my cock, and then back up at me. "But not if you're uncomfortable with it." She offers me a tentative smile.

Uncomfortable? With the idea of burying myself in my perfect little human woman?

I snatch her up off the ground in one swoop, and she squeaks as I settle her in the cradle of my arms. I glare down at her.

"I am *not* going to have you here in the pine needles," I snarl. "We are going home."

Maisie clings to my neck, but her eyes are shining. "Okay. Take me home, then."

I spread my wings out behind me, beat them against the air, and shoot off into the night sky.

Maisie

Flying is really, really cool. Nobody has any idea just how cool it is because, well, most people can't just spread their wings and *fly*.

But my guy can.

I hold tight to Barnaby as trees rush beneath us, not because I'm afraid he'll drop me, but because I'm afraid I might float out of his arms. His wings beat again and again, a steady, rhythmic sound as he carries us toward the mansion.

I can't believe what we're about to do. I rub my thighs together because I'm already wet between the legs. As if Barnaby can smell it, his lip quirks. It's strange, and strangely lovely, to see his true form's face. It still reminds me of my vampire in his human form, just changed. Different.

Good different. *Hot* different.

And I clearly blew his mind when I sucked his dick. I wonder what other ways I can blow his mind.

The mansion comes into view and Barnaby swoops down, making a straight line for the front door. He doesn't release me as he wiggles the knob open with his clawed hand, then bends his neck to squeeze inside the doorframe.

Oh, boy. He's really big. I hope this actually works.

Still carrying me bridal-style, Barnaby rushes up the steps of the house and ducks into one of the guest rooms. I still haven't seen his coffin yet, but I hope I do someday.

Though he sets me down gently on the bed, all the muscles in Barnaby's body are coiled tight and his cock still lurks at half-mast. I sit up on my knees, watching him as I pull my shirt over my head and toss it away. Barnaby's long, black tongue darts out to lick his lips as I unhook my bra, too.

I want him to know just how beautiful he is in any form. How much I want him, no matter what he looks like. The horns and wings and enormous cock are a bonus, though.

I make quick work of my corduroys and underwear, throwing them onto the floor with the rest of it. When I'm naked at last, I gesture for Barnaby to come closer. I don't even think he realizes he's been gently stroking his cock while he watches me, and now it's thick, swollen, and alert for me.

"Maisie." My name comes out of his mouth in a hoarse, growling whisper. "Do you know what you ask for?"

Instead of answering, I spread my thighs on the bed and reach down between my legs. Barnaby gasps as I run my finger down over my clit, touching it while I stare at him. He takes a step closer, then another one, each *thump!* of his heavy, clawed feet on the floor making me wetter and more excited for what's to come. I move my fingers faster, then raise my other hand to touch my nipple.

Barnaby groans and presses a huge knee down onto the bed next to me. I quicken my pace, rolling over my clit again and again while he pants over me.

"I didn't think it could be any bigger," I say between labored breaths as I watch him stroke himself, "but I was wrong."

It does not seem to amuse him. If anything, Barnaby shrinks back, and his hand slows down.

"I don't want to hurt you." He fixes me with that glowing stare. "I will never hurt you."

"Then I guess you'd better get me good and ready." I dip two fingers inside myself, and Barnaby's breaths speed up as his eyes dart down between my legs. "Before you fuck me."

A low, rumbling growl slips out of his mouth. He grabs my hand and pulls it away, bringing my fingers up to his lips. He licks me and groans at the taste.

Before I can blink, Barnaby is on his knees, shoving my thighs apart. He buries his mouth in my pussy, and he's never eaten me out like this before, not ever. His incredibly long tongue attacks my clit, spinning me up into a raging-hot inferno before ducking down lower, where he presses it inside me. It's large and thick, and I wriggle as he fucks it in and out of me.

"Barnaby!" I reach down to grab his hair like I usually do, but my hands find his massive horns there instead. Gripping them tight, I gyrate my hips against his face as he torments me with his tongue. Before I know it, my entire body is shaking, and then I'm drowning in my bliss.

Claws grip the flesh of my ass as I climax, and I scream out Barnaby's name. He keeps frantically licking me as I cool down until I'm writhing and whimpering. When he rises above me again, Barnaby grabs his giant cock and strokes it once, hard, earning droplets of cum at the tip.

"Please," I whine, curling my toes around his hips to draw him in. Barnaby sucks in a breath, and those glowing eyes are hooded.

"Tell me to stop if it doesn't fit," he says in a somber tone, and I nod quickly.

"Go slow."

He kisses my forehead, but before he can pull away, I take him by the cheeks and pull him down toward me. Then I plant my mouth on his, even though the shape is strange, making sure he knows just how fucking hot he is—just how much I want him.

Barnaby gasps in surprise, then after a moment to collect himself, begins kissing me back in earnest. But instead of pushing me to the bed, as I'd hoped, he pulls away and sits down against the headboard, spreading his odd legs out in front of him. His cock stands up straight, his rather copious balls hanging beneath it.

"This way," Barnaby says, his voice barely more than a whisper, "you can take me how you want."

I shiver all over. It makes sense, actually, and it's incredible that this massive monster is ready for *me* to take *him*.

I nod rapidly and climb up, straddling his waist with my knees. His cock juts up between us, leaking for me, hungry for me. I sit high so I'm now raised above him, and slowly guide him between my legs. That veined cock throbs in my hand as I rub against it, letting his head stimulate me, circling my hips to grind us together. Barnaby clenches the comforter with his claws.

Slipping my hand underneath his, I lift it and settle it on my waist so he's holding me instead.

I lean forward and position the massive, sloped head of his cock right at the juncture of my thighs, where I'm warm and wet for him.

"Hold me," I tell him, memorizing the planes of his strange, beautiful face, committing the horns and the wings folded behind him to memory.

Nodding obediently, Barnaby leaves one clawed hand on my hip, raising the other to my breast. He surrounds it, brushing his claw over the nipple, and I feel myself clenching right where I want him.

With a deep breath, I sink down onto him.

Chapter Nineteen

Barnaby

OH, SHE IS MUCH too small.

Maisie didn't hide her surprise the first time she saw me without my trousers on, even in my human form, and that effect is only magnified by the sheer size of my true form.

Has any vampire in this shape taken a human this way? Is it possible? Am I going to split her in half?

The head of my cock vanishes inside her, and I can only stare as she brings me in. Almost immediately, though, her body halts, and Maisie inhales sharply. The last thing I want is to harm her or tear her.

But I trust her to know what she can take.

Maisie lifts herself up, then sinks down again, swallowing more of me this time. Her warm heat welcomes me, and I can't help the groan that's yanked from my lips as she presses down harder, more of my length disappearing into her. She's so plush and soaked inside that my true form is already struggling not to grab her, shove her down on the bed and rut into her roughly. But that's why I put her on top, so that I couldn't have that power.

Instead I grip her ass with my claws, trying not to pierce her soft skin, and let my head fall back. The clench of her is almost too powerful, and it's going to take all my self-control not to explode inside her yet. I try to slow my breathing as Maisie rises again, and then slowly lowers herself onto me, her channel somehow giving to allow even more of me inside her.

"Maisie," I moan helplessly, the pleasure almost sweeping me under. Of their own accord, my hips buck upwards, driving even more of myself into her soft cunt, and she moans in response. When I look down, she's taken more than half of me, and I can't believe this small, precious human is actually doing this, on top of me, sucking my cock inside her while I'm in my horrifying true form.

My human is a gift. She is everything to me, and I know for certain now that I cannot possibly let her go.

And then, by some marvel of the universe, Maisie sinks down even more. Her cry of pleasure travels from my neck down my spine, and I almost come apart at the feel of her all around me, embracing me and squeezing me so delightfully. I sit further forward so I can retake her lips in mine, and she moans so prettily as I assume the heavy lifting, picking her up by the ass with one hand and teasing her nipple with the other as my hips thrust upward.

"You feel so good," Maisie murmurs against my lips, and my wings can't help but unfold behind me, my whole body reveling in her praise. "Barnaby, fuck. Ah!"

She collapses against me like a puppet with cut strings as I fuck into her again, and again, and again. I hold her that way, cradling her to my chest as I take over, sliding in and out, my cock drenched in how wet she is, my bollocks seizing and trembling as I get closer and closer to my finish.

I need to make her come first, though, but I can't do that in this position. Now that I'm well seated inside her, I wrap my arms around her back and flip us both over, so she's lying on the bed and I'm crouched over her, her legs spread around my waist. I hike one of her knees up over my arm, where my blood has already dried, then bring my finger down to her clit. Unfortunately, I have rather long claws in this form, and I don't want to hurt her.

"Damn." I curl my finger to use my knuckle instead. That works just as well, and when I start thrusting inside Maisie and attacking her clit at the same time, her eyes grow huge.

"Barnaby...!" She gasps and throws her head back, letting out a sharp cry when I plunge into her. I'm still shocked at how much of me she can take—not my whole shaft, but most of it. The sight of her cunt stretched wide around my cock nearly carries me over the edge.

"You're so beautiful," I whisper to her, snapping my hips faster as Maisie's channel squeezes tighter and tighter around me. She's close, I can tell. I long to let it take over, to burst inside her and fill her until my seed is dripping out of her, but I manage to rein it in a few moments longer.

"Barnaby." Maisie's cry is hoarse and addled with her pleasure. "I... I..." She cries out as I sink deep, then reel my hips back again. "I think I love you."

The declaration takes me by surprise. She loves me? Even when I am like *this*?

Emotion washes over me in a powerful wave. I've never met a woman like Maisie before, and I never will again. I know the truth immediately, that I would do absolutely anything for her.

I lean down until we're face to face, and continue pumping my hips, finding my home inside her over and over again.

"Maisie," I say with a severe certainty. "I love you. I love you so much." I'm close, and changing position is bringing her closer, too. She writhes with every thrust, her whole body tensing underneath me. I grit my teeth to hold off as her cries climb in volume and her blood thunders through her body, so sweet and so pure. My fangs slide even further out of their sheaths, ready to drink from her.

"Do it," she moans, clutching me with fingers like claws. "Bite me. Drink from me, Barnaby!"

How can I resist her commanding me that way?

Opening my mouth wide, I wrap my teeth around her throat and sink them in. Her hot, wet blood immediately pools on my tongue and I rapidly suck it down, the perfect nectar filling my body with a new, powerful strength and resilience.

Not that it matters when Maisie screams my name, her hands gripping me like claws, and clamps down tight around me.

Maisie

Nothing in the entire world could feel like Barnaby inside me, his fangs buried in my neck. The sharp pain blends viscerally with the pleasure, and it hurls me right into the most powerful climax I've ever had in my life.

That thick cock swells as my body squeezes, and my bliss completely overwhelms me. Barnaby's eyes grow huge and his mouth falls open, my blood dripping from his fangs. Once more he thrusts inside me, spinning my orgasm even higher, and he bellows as he meets his own finish.

Hot cum shoots inside me so powerfully that I can feel it filling every small gap that's left. Barnaby snarls like an animal as he pumps again, unleashing even more.

And then, finally, our bodies cool enough that he relaxes, lowering himself so his nose touches the tip of mine. His lids hang low over his red eyes, his expression soft with his satisfaction. He nuzzles me, stroking the sides of my body with his clawed hands.

"Maisie," he murmurs, cradling me close to him. "Did you mean what you said?"

I can't help a satisfied yawn. "About what?"

"How you feel about me. Was that just a moment of passion?"

I push him away enough that I can peer up into his face.

"Of course I meant it." I cradle his cheek in my palm. "You mean so much to me. The fact that you showed me this—that you *made love to me* like this, in the form you feared so much, gives me so much trust and faith in you."

And it's true. He showed me all of himself, gave me everything he is, and I love all of it even more.

Barnaby

Her words crash over me in a tidal wave. How does this human woman understand me so well? How does she know that, though I appear strong in this form, I'm truly at my most vulnerable?

"I love you." Maisie repeats it with a powerful certainty. "I've loved you for a while now, but this confirms what I already knew."

I sigh, playing with her red ringlets. "Thank you." I kiss her face all over—her cheeks, her nose, her lips. "I love you, too. And I don't know if—"

I cut myself off, unwilling to say what I really, truly feel. That I want her to stay with me. That I want to be wherever she is. That I don't know if I'll survive her leaving me.

"What is it?" she asks as I slowly withdraw from her, and my spend gushes out of her onto the bed. I generated quite a lot in this form.

"You are leaving." I state it as a fact. She does not have long here. "You will be leaving me behind."

Her mouth bobs open. "Oh." Then, to my surprise, she wraps her arms around my neck and tugs me down close to her. I don't resist as I rest my face in the crook of her neck.

"I don't want to," she whispers. "I don't want to leave you, not ever."

"Then don't!" I sit up abruptly, my wings beating the air as they extend out behind me. Suddenly I am overcome with such a fury, such a determination, that I will *not* let her go. "Please, Maisie. Stay. I will install internet here at the manse. I'll do whatever you need to—"

She sits up, too, and fiercely presses her mouth to mine.

"Barnaby," she says between kisses, "you don't have to convince me. I want to stay. I want to be with you." Then she pulls away, and her gaze drops to her lap. "But... what about you?"

I don't understand the question. "What about me?"

"Whatever we decide to do, you're... you're going to outlive me. I will die someday, and you won't. You can't."

I don't know why this thought hadn't crossed my mind when I asked her to be with me. Of course I'll outlive her mortal life, and mine will continue into forever.

My heart breaks at the thought. I would come to love her even more over the years, and her death would destroy me, even more than Beatrice's did. I would lose yet more of my family, the only family I have.

As this sadness wells up in me, my true form fades, my wings receding into stubs along with my horns. My bones shrink to accommodate my human shape. Soon I am myself again, naked on top of her, and I lie down at her side.

"I can die," I tell her at last, rolling over so I'm facing her. "Perhaps the one myth that's true about us. We become mortal if we are staked, or if we are burned. Then we can die."

Her expression is horrified. "Barnaby! That's terrible!"

"It would mean I didn't have to live without you."

Tears well up in her big eyes, and she embraces me with her whole body. I feel wet droplets against my chest, and I wish I hadn't said it.

Then Maisie's muffled voice rises to my ears. "What if you turned me?"

"What?" Just the words stir fear and nausea in me. "I can't do that to you. I can't doom you to this life, too."

She lifts her head. "Doom me? You would be blessing me. You would be giving me all of time with you." She smiles. "Oh my gosh, I could do so *much*. I could finish my game and make more games. Maybe I could even own my own company!"

How she can regard the idea of becoming like me so callously, so easily, disturbs me.

"You don't know what you're asking," I say in a low voice.

"I do." She smiles up at me, running her hand through my hair. "Then I could be with you forever."

Chapter Twenty

Maisie

HE DOESN'T BELIEVE ME, but he'll have to. I want that life with him, a life where we could do this dance forever.

"But you'll become a monster like me," he says, shaking his head. "I would be sentencing you to this."

I shrug. "Then I could protect you, too, like you protected me tonight."

He searches my face, as if nothing I'm saying makes sense.

"You would do that?" His voice trembles. "For me?"

"For us." I hug him tightly, and Barnaby relaxes into my touch. "Though my parents might be a little mad."

"Let's wait and see," he says, stroking my back. "Move in with me. Set up your business here. Make sure that this is what you want, and in a few years, we will reconsider."

I sigh. "Fine. But I'm not letting this go."

He chuckles. "I don't imagine you will."

The next morning, I'm quite sore, and Barnaby inspects me to make sure he hasn't torn me with his true form's monstrous cock. I'm intact, but I think I'll need a break for a few days before we can do it again.

When we walk back to my car, the werewolf is gone.

"I'm going to have to deal with that," Barnaby grumbles. "Or somebody will."

We drive into town together, and he opens the store while I head back up to my apartment and immediately start packing my things. We decided we won't bother waiting, not when we spend every night together, anyway.

When I finally get to my computer, I open it up and check my email. There's a new message from Wade... from two days ago.

Has it really been that long since I logged on? I've been so wrapped up in Barnaby that I hadn't even seen it.

"Call me," is all the email says, and a shudder travels through me. Is this good news, or bad news? Am I losing my job, or keeping it?

I'm surprised to find this email doesn't stir that deep dread in me I expected. If I get to keep my job, I'll be ecstatic—but it won't be the end of the world if I lose it, either. Now I have a life here, and Barnaby will be there to catch me if I fall.

After tidying my mussed hair, I get on video chat and call. Wade answers, and to my surprise, he's smiling.

"Maisie! I hope you've been enjoying your vacation."

I hesitate, unsure how much to tell him. "It's been, um, surprisingly good."

"Good! I hadn't heard from you in a few days, so I assumed you were off having fun. Well, the investigation has concluded, and I wanted to tell you..."

My heart thunders in my chest.

"...that you've been cleared of all wrongdoing. It was a bug in the deployment system, which you don't work on. It took us a long time to find it, though, and I'm sorry about that." His mouth screws up like he's swallowed a lemon. "I shouldn't have blamed you."

It wasn't me. It really wasn't me. I didn't fail, and I didn't fuck up.

I drop my head into my hands as relief washes over me.

"Maisie?" Wade asks, and I glance up at the screen. "Are you ready to come back to work tomorrow?"

"Yes!" I sit up in my chair. This is what I've been wanting for weeks now, and it's finally here. "Yes, please. I'd love that."

"All right. Well, head home tonight and we'll get you up and running again."

I don't have to think about it. "I'm not going home. I'm staying here."

"What? Where are you?"

I explain about the little town of Hallow's Cove, and how I've fallen in love with it. "I met someone," I say sheepishly. "And I want to... stay here. To be with him."

Wade grins. "Well, then. You already work remotely, so I don't see why that would be a problem." He smacks his desk. "Good for you, Maisie. But you said it's a monster town, didn't you? So who...?"

He doesn't finish asking the question. I laugh at his awkwardness.

"A vampire," I say. "He's a good guy. A little grumpy at first, but I think we've gotten past that hurdle." Barnaby was simply glowing this morning, all smiles, and I love seeing him that way.

Wade laughs. "All right then. Maisie's going to marry a vampire. That wasn't on my bingo card."

"*Marry?*" I think about this for a moment. Yes, I've agreed to stay. But marriage? That hadn't landed on my radar yet.

But if Barnaby asked me, I'd say yes in a heartbeat.

"Let me know when the wedding is," Wade says, smirking, "and the team will come, I'm sure."

"I'll tell you as soon as it happens."

With that, we end the call, and I get back to packing up my belongings. Then, while I wait for Barnaby to finish his workday, I binge the rest of the Anne Hadron novel.

And damn, it's good. The heroine travels all across Europe, searching for the meaning in the next stage of her life. Eventually, she meets another woman about the same age in Austria, and a story of self-discovery turns into a love story.

By the end of it I'm in tears, flipping the pages to find out what happens next. It has a bittersweet ending when her lover passes away, but that doesn't bother me. I like a little complexity.

It's the author's note that catches my attention. "This book is dedicated to the women who inspired the story," it reads. "While I have fictionalized many of the events in this novel, it all stems from a true tale that's close to my heart."

The women who inspired the story? I didn't realize that Anne Hadron was inspired by real events. I wonder who her subjects were when they lived.

Finally, I close the last page and wipe my face. Then I rush down to the bookstore, and Barnaby gets to his feet when I run inside in a jingle of bells. I slap the novel down on the counter, tears still in my eyes.

"Maisie...?" he asks, his expression uncertain.

"Give me the next one!" I slide the book across to him, and his mouth transforms into a grin.

"I have every book she's published," he says, as if to reassure me. He plucks one off the front display and hands it to me.

"Don't you want me to pay?" I ask.

Barnaby gives me a stunned look. "Why would I make my girlfriend pay for a book?"

I snort at this. Somehow, *girlfriend* and *boyfriend* feel like ridiculous titles for whatever it is we have.

"All right. I'll accept your generosity this time." I sweep the new book up into my arms. "I'm all finished packing when you're done here. And..." I have a huge smile pasted on my face. "I talked to Wade. The investigation concluded that what happened wasn't my fault."

His mouth falls open. "It wasn't?"

"Nope. And I have my job back!"

Barnaby's eyes light up. He hops off his stool and jogs with a rather youthful vigor around the counter, then tangles me up in his arms. I spot Mayor Louise pass by the front window, and she has a huge, shit-eating grin on her face. She gives me a brief little wave before moving on.

"I'm so happy for you," he says, leaning down to peck my lips. "Everything turned out just how it was supposed to."

"I'll need to drive back home at some point to get the rest of my things and move out of my apartment," I say as Barnaby releases me.

He nods rapidly. "I'll go with you on my next day off."

"You'll leave Hallow's Cove?"

He shrugs. "It's not ideal, but I imagine you'll have a lot of belongings you want to move."

That's true. I could use some help. I want my nice desk, and I know exactly where it will go in the manse.

"All right then. It's settled." I kiss his cheek. "Thank you. I'll see you when you close up."

Barnaby pushes a lock of my hair behind my ear. "I can't wait."

When I get back to my apartment, I stack up my new books, excited to dive into them. But I have something to take care of first. I open a new email and, after some deep-dive internet sleuthing, I find Anne Hadron's direct email address.

Dear Ms. Hadron,
I read your latest novel, The Knowing and the Finding, *and it mesmerized me. My boyfriend, Barnaby Hallow, is a huge fan of yours, and a bookstore owner here in Hallow's Cove. Might you be passing through this area sometime in the future? We would love to host you for a signing event. I know that meeting you would mean the world to him.*
Best regards,
Maisie Robbins

I send the email, hoping Barnaby won't mind. I don't expect a response, but it would be a pleasant surprise if I got one.

Barnaby

That afternoon, I call up Mayor Louise and tell her all about the werewolf we encountered. I don't reveal, of course, how my true form emerged to solve the problem. Maisie knows his name after encountering him before at Killy's, and Louise pledges to find him. We can't have a vicious creature like that out and about during tourist season, but perhaps he can find support and prevent another full-moon rampage.

That evening, when the sun has long set, we load Maisie's few bags into the back of her car and drive to the manse. She's still a little sore, so we settle for licking and sucking on one another until we're both shivering and spent. She lets me bite her, which sates my need for now.

"If I turn," Maisie says with a forlorn face, "then you can't drink my blood anymore."

I cock my head at her. "Vampires drink from one another all the time. I would say it's even more delightful, and it gives us greater strength."

Now, she's simply glowing. "So I wouldn't have to drink cow's blood? Because that shit looked gross."

I burst out laughing. How long has it been since I laughed this way? Since before Eleanor, I know that.

"No. You wouldn't have to drink cow's blood as long as you have me."

She sighs in relief. "Good."

After she's had a good meal, Maisie follows me down into the basement, and I show her my coffin. I lie down in it, and she crawls in beside me, molding her body to mine as I close the lid.

A few days later is the next street fair, and as agreed, I open the antique shop for visitors. I grumble as children enter despite the signage out front, and I follow them around the room like a hawk to make sure they don't knock over any of my vintage lamps.

It's a very popular attraction, though, and something about seeing all my furniture in broad daylight makes the specter of my memories much smaller. Someone even offers me a good chunk of money for a matching chair and nightstand. I hadn't considered selling any of it, but the man plans on surprising his wife with the set, so I agree to his price.

I know what it's like to want to see your woman smile.

When I look up, I find Maisie grinning at me from where she's lounging on a sofa. She exchanges a few whispered words with the mayor, which I don't particularly love, but I'm glad she's finding friends here.

By the time afternoon has turned into evening, the tourists have petered off, and we close the antique shop for the night. But Maisie is bouncing up and down, clearly excited to tell me something.

"What is it?" I finally ask, amused by her impatience.

"Well..." She scratches the back of her head. "I reached out to Anne Hadron. I asked her if she would consider doing a signing here."

My mouth falls open. Anne Hadron? *Here?*

"Don't panic," she says with a laugh. "She said no. It's too far for her to travel, and she's getting on in years. But..." Maisie opens her laptop and turns it toward me. "It's as I suspected."

I take the laptop and read the email on the screen.

Dear Maisie,

Thank you for reaching out to me. It is interesting that you mention Barnaby Hallow. Agatha, the love interest in The Knowing and the Finding, *is based on a real person. I discovered her diary in an archive, and that is how the novel was born.*

*Her name was Beatrice Hallow. She had a long and
fascinating life and died in the arms of her lover.
I thought perhaps Barnaby would want to know.*
Best,
Anne

My throat constricts. Suddenly, the details click together. How Agatha had a twin brother. How some event in her past had broken her heart, but her relationship with the heroine had helped heal her.

My sister. She lived a long life. She found love. She died happy.

I don't realize there are tears falling from my eyes until I hear Maisie whisper, "Oh, Barnaby." She takes the laptop and sets it down so she can wrap me up in her arms.

Beatrice. After a century of mourning, of never knowing what became of her, I finally cry. It rushes out of me like a waterfall after a dam breaks, but Maisie is there with me the whole time.

At least now I know, and I can properly grieve her.

Some days later, we trek to Maisie's apartment in the city, as much as it makes me uncomfortable to leave the familiarity of Hallow's Cove. When we return with all of Maisie's belongings loaded into a truck, Rick joins us to help unload it and set it up in one of my many guest rooms, which has already been converted into an office for Maisie.

As we settle into our new life, though, one last concern lingers in the back of my mind.

A few weeks later, after Maisie has moaned underneath me and let me drink from her again, I cage her in with my arms and kiss her on the lips.

"Beloved," I say quietly. "May I ask you something?"

She nods sleepily. "Whatever you want."

"Will you be my wife?"

Her eyes fly open, and she blinks at me a few times as if processing what I just asked.

"Are you saying you want to marry me?" She sits up abruptly, bonking me in the nose with her forehead. I rub it and she apologizes profusely.

"Of course I want to marry you. You fill my life with love. You complete me."

"Yes!" She throws her arms around me, and I catch her in my lap. "Yes, I want to marry you and be your wife and live here forever and ever!"

I wonder how exactly I got so lucky as to find this woman. Or rather, that she found me.

It's a small ceremony, with Maisie's family and friends on one side, and my few friends on the other. I like to imagine that Beatrice is here with me in spirit, seeing that I have found my way back to the light after all.

Maisie's family finds it odd that she's decided to move here, and with a vampire no less, but they are surprisingly accepting. They just seem happy that she's found someone to love, and I'm glad that she has such sweet parents. Her little brother is nothing but overjoyed and welcomes me happily into the family.

After the ceremony, I find that our small reception has grown rather large thanks to Mayor Louise telling everyone about it. Ted from the diner has provided the food, and Harley the drinks.

That night, Maisie and I dance together in front of everyone, and I can't help but admire her in her beautiful white dress.

"Thank you," I murmur in her ear as I hold her close to me, our feet moving in unison. "For loving me."

"Always," she says, kissing my cheek. "So now, are you going to turn me? So I can love you forever?"

I have to laugh. She is relentless.

"Soon," I tell her. "We should find you a good coffin first, though."

"Just please don't make me dig myself out. I would cry like a baby."

I shake my head. "Don't worry. It will be painful, but I'll make it as easy for you as possible." I can't believe she wants to give me such a gift.

We dance the night away, and then, when all the guests have left, I take her home to the manse and make love to her long into the early hours of the morning, promising her an eternity together.

Chapter Twenty-One

Epilogue

Maisie

"Oh, I ʟɪᴋᴇ ᴛʜɪs one!" I skid to a stop next to a coffin with a reddish-pink hue to the wood. The inside is lined with soft, cream-colored silk, and it's probably out of our price range, but I instantly fall in love with it.

Barnaby hums, stopping next to me to examine it. He smooths his hand over the lining, squishing the padding.

"This would be comfortable enough," he says. "What do you think?"

"I should try it out first." I wave over the salesman, an unfortunately average human who has no idea why we're here. "Excuse me, can I please get into this one?"

He stares at me. "Get... into it?"

"Yeah, I want to see how comfy it is."

His eyes widen, and he glances between Barnaby and me. The nearest funeral home is outside of Hallow's Cove, so we had to make a little trek to a human-occupied town to shop for my new coffin.

"Sure, I guess so," the salesman says.

He watches with concern as I climb into the coffin, then slide down so I'm fitted neatly in the silk padding. I close my eyes and let myself relax into it, imagining myself sleeping here every night.

"I need a pillow," I tell Barnaby, cracking one eye open.

He nods. "We'll get you a nice one."

When I'm finished, I climb back out. "This one's good," I say. "Comfortable, cozy, and pretty to look at."

The salesman's mouth falls open as I pat the lid.

"How much?" I ask, but just as he's about to reply, Barnaby holds up a hand to stop him.

"It doesn't matter. I have the funds. I want you to be happy with your choice, Maisie."

I stand up on my toes to kiss his cheek. "Thank you, love."

The salesman rings us up and promises to call when my coffin is ready. People don't usually take theirs home with them, but he agrees to it anyway. We'll come back in a few weeks with Barnaby's Wagoneer to pick it up.

I'm nearly bursting with excitement as we drive home to Hallow's Cove. Barnaby is going to turn me soon, and though there are things I'll miss—mostly coffee, pie, and potato chips—it'll all be worth it in the end if it means I can spend centuries, maybe even millennia with my husband.

I shiver all over. It's still new, but every time I think about it, it makes me even more excited for our life together. Barnaby is mine and I'm his, and soon we'll seal it with our blood.

Still, as much as I love him, I make sure to take time for myself. Sometimes on the weekends I carry the latest book Barnaby's gotten in stock up the mountain, and find a nice place to sit at the very top of Twilight Peak while I read. The view is phenomenal from up here, and sometimes I pause just to eat an apple and look out over Hallow's Cove—my home.

One night, as we curl up together in front of the fire with me on his lap, Barnaby brings out a new book I haven't seen before. It's a modern book, which is very unlike him.

"I thought this might help," he says as he holds it up in front of me. The title reads: *Beginning Your Life as a Vampire.* "I never had anything like this when I was turned, but I thought it might help you prepare. Those first few years are tough, and even though I'll be here to support you, this might give you some additional tools to make the transition easier."

I sweep the book up into my hands, marveling at the thoughtfulness of it.

"Thank you." I kiss his cheek and rub my nose against him. "Thank you so much."

Barnaby

It is, as I expected, a difficult ordeal to turn Maisie. If I hadn't checked in with her many times over the last year, I would still be unsure of whether it was the right decision—but even after the thirteen-month probation period I suggested when we first married, she's intent on her goal and I have no reason not to help her achieve it.

Besides, I have my own selfish incentives. I love her with all my heart, body, and soul, and I never want to say goodbye to her. Now we can spend forever together, and I expect we'll discover even more new and interesting ways to express our feelings over time. I have some ideas that involve hot wax.

It's frightening to nearly drain Maisie dry, and it makes me as swollen as a mosquito. When she's just barely clinging to life, her face pale and her breaths shallow, I bite into my wrist and feed her. Gladly she drinks of me, which is its own kind of erotic.

And then, she dies.

Horror descends on me as Maisie's pulse stops and her eyes turn glassy. Have I made a mistake? Have I lost her?

I panic, but Adeline is there to calm me down and help me move Maisie into her coffin. Now it's time to wait.

I sit by Maisie's side all night and then all the next day, my leg bouncing with fear and anticipation. I don't remember how many days and nights it took for me to awaken—because, well, I was dead—but surely it shouldn't be this long.

Then, I hear a tapping on the coffin.

"Barnaby!" a frightened voice calls out from inside. "Barnaby, help!"

Frantically I open the lid, and there's my wife, her skin paler than before, though still covered in freckles. I gasp in relief and pull her out, into my lap.

"God, I'm so hungry," is the very first thing she says, her new fangs extruding from her gums. "Holy shit, I'm *starving!*"

That is just the beginning.

Those first few months are as challenging for Maisie as I expected. She thirsts for fresh blood constantly. I do my best to feed her myself, supplementing with animal blood, but it's not enough. She cries at night sometimes, asking when the craving will go away.

"It never truly does," I tell her as she sits in my lap by the fire, and I stroke her brilliant red hair. "But the ache will fade with time, and meanwhile, you always have me."

She settles back into the circle of my arms, her nose pressing into my throat. She inhales, her whole body going taut, and it's almost instantaneous that my cock comes to life. There's nothing it loves more than being inside her.

"Maisie," I murmur, my hand trailing down her shoulder to her breasts, where I cup one in my hand. "I think you ought to get on the chair now, so I can eat."

She giggles, knowing just what I mean. We trade places so now she's sitting in my armchair, and her breaths are already coming faster. I unbutton her jeans, then slide them down her legs until I can toss them aside. But her sweet center is still hiding from me inside her cute underwear, so I shimmy those down, too.

Once upon a time I might have folded her clothes before setting them aside, but I'm too hungry for Maisie.

I pull her legs apart and dive in, sweeping my tongue all the way from her slit to her clit just so I can taste her. She sinks back into the chair, her hips sliding closer to me, and I lick even more frantically as her quick breaths become gasps, and then moans. It's easy to fit two fingers inside her—given that I make love to her twice a day at least—which catapults her moans into cries of ecstasy.

"Barnaby!" Her wet heat clutches me tight. "Ah!"

I moan, too, as I pump my fingers inside her, imagining how it will be my cock soon. Then she hits her peak, and her release trickles down my hand.

I love making her come more than anything.

"That was so good," Maisie whispers, still breathing heavily. "But I need something else now."

I know just what my woman wants. I undress in front of her, her eyes drinking me up while I remove each layer—my vest, my tie, my shirt and pants. When I'm finally naked, she has a broad smile on her lips.

Now it's my turn to sit in the chair, my cock poking straight up between my legs. Maisie crawls onto my lap, pushing me down so my shaft brushes over her wet sex. She rubs us together, and my senses are already so heightened that this simple contact is driving me wild.

"Maisie." My voice is strained. "I need to be inside you. Now."

With a mischievous grin, she lifts herself up and positions my cock right at the crux of her thighs. Then, ever so slowly, she sinks down onto me.

I let out a thick moan as she easily swallows me up, taking me deep into her body. I'll never stop marveling at how wonderfully warm she is, how well she fits me. Maisie rises to her knees again, changing her angle as she brings me inside her a second time.

Her eyes roll back in her head. "You feel so good," she moans.

I give her a mischievous smirk. "You know what would feel even better?" I run my hands up from her belly to her breasts, cupping them in my hands before plucking her nipples.

"Wh-what?" she asks, breathless as she impales herself on me again.

It's easy to summon the monster, as it always lurks close by when I'm naked with Maisie. Hers comes out from time to time, too, and more than once we've made love high in the sky above the manse, both our sets of wings flapping.

Eagerly, my true form rises to the surface, my bones stretching, my face changing—and most importantly, my cock swelling and lengthening.

"Oh, fuck," Maisie moans as she gets even tighter around my increasing size. "Yes!" She pulls me in close to her as she continues fucking me. Her lips find mine, and it will never cease to amaze me that not only does she not find this form horrifying, but it turns her on.

As her pleasure takes her over and her thighs wear out, Maisie's thrusts slow down. I pick her up by the ass, still sunk deep inside her, and flip us over. Now she's on her back on my chair, her legs wrapped around my waist as my instincts take over.

I plow into her mercilessly, overcome with need. She clutches me even tighter against her as her fangs emerge.

"Barnaby," she whimpers, her whole body shaking underneath mine as she approaches her climax. "Barnaby, please!"

I lean down and tilt my neck so she has easier access, and she buries her fangs into my flesh.

That's all it takes. The sharp bite and the instantaneous burst of pleasure meld together, and soon I'm roaring, plunging inside her as all my muscles bunch up tight.

"You taste so good," she moans, licking my blood off her lips. Her cunt is squeezing me, daring me to go off inside her.

"And you feel incredible." I nuzzle her nose with mine. "My love. My wife."

I lean down toward her own exposed throat, open my mouth, and bite her.

Her orgasm is instantaneous. Maisie lets out a full-throated scream as I suck on her, devouring her, all her perfect, hot blood fueling me even more. I fuck her with even more muscle, using all the strength in my true form, and Maisie's head falls back as she comes a second time.

Finally, I can't hold off any longer. I sink into her once more, and as I meet my own powerful finish, everything spurts out of me. I groan as I nearly collapse on top of her.

Maisie smiles warmly at me, her mouth red with my blood. She kisses my lips again as she tangles her hands in my hair.

"I love you," she whispers.

Still buried in her warm depths, I hug her back with all my might.

"You mean the world to me, Maisie."

We lounge in the soft, warm fog of our lovemaking for some time before finding our way to our coffins, where we say goodnight.

As I pull the lid shut, I never could have believed I'd find a happiness like this one, where I could love someone so fully and she would love me in return, until the end of time.

* * *

Thank you for reading!

If you liked this book, please remember to leave a review on your preferred sites to help other readers find my work.

First and foremost, I want to thank my readers for giving this book a chance. I would also like to thank Chocological for the gorgeous cover illustration, and my editor Emily Michel for always catching my bad comma placements. To my critique partners, especially Carlotta Page, who gave me phenomenal feedback: You all make this possible. And of course, I want to thank my amazing spouse, who has always supported my dreams—and given me lots of inspiration for my characters' sexy adventures.I couldn't have done this without the expertise of my fellow self-published romance authors. Thank you for inviting me into your circles and helping me through this process. I couldn't have done it without you.

Hallow's Cove

Looking for more adventures in Hallow's Cove? Here are the next books in the series...

Going Au Naturale by L.E. Eldridge
Love is Trash by Emily Antionette
Gaming with the Gargoyle by Kass O'Shire
When Mermaids Fly by Allegra Hall
Screwed by the Minotaur by Jenifer Wood
Wolves and Whipped Cream by Ash Raven
Snowed In by Petra Palerno

Also by Lyonne Riley

Trollkin Lovers

Stealing the Troll's Heart
Healing the Orc's Heart
Capturing the Orc's Heart
Charming the Troll's Heart
Keeping the Human's Heart
Finding the Troll's Heart
Tempting the Ogre's Heart
Enchanting the Ogre's Heart
Knowing the Ogre's Heart

DreamTogether Breeding Program

Bred by the Wolfman
Bred by the Dragon

Anthologies

The Monster Menagerie

Standalones

Prince of Beasts
Programmed for Love
My Minotaur Husband
Seduced by The Werewolves
Five Gifts for the Blacksmith's Wife

About the Author

Lyonne Riley spends most of her time writing fantastical, monstrous, and super steamy books. She lives in a small town in the middle of nowhere with her spouse and two dogs.

For all the latest regarding books, and to get a FREE Trollkin Lovers novella, join her newsletter! You can also find signed paperbacks and artwork of your favorite books.

www.LyonneRiley.com